A BUBBLE GARDEN

URSULA HOLDEN

METHUEN

First published in Great Britain 1989
by Methuen London
81 Fulham Road, London SW3 6RB
Copyright © 1989 by Ursula Holden

British Library Cataloguing in Publication Data

Holden, Ursula
A bubble garden.
I. Title
823'.914 [F]

ISBN 0 413 19610 0

Photoset, printed and bound in Great Britain
by Redwood Burn Limited, Trowbridge, Wiltshire

'I'm Forever Blowing Bubbles'
© 1919 B. Feldman & Co Ltd
Reproduced by permission of
EMI Music Publishing Ltd,
London WC2H OLD
and Redwood Music Ltd,
129 Park Street, London W1X 3FA

To Paul Sheridan

A BUBBLE GARDEN

ONE

Everything that had happened to him before Bonnie was a foretaste, marking time, so it seemed. His childhood, his adolescence, his move from Streatham to Clerkenwell before his war service all led up to him meeting her. His real life started in Ireland when he'd seen his dear one.

He had never been there before, the thought made him sentimental. He would see that green grass, drink their Guinness, hear talk of leprechauns. The people there were amazingly kind, known for their welcome.

His invitation was timed perfectly. A civilian again after his army demob, he hadn't yet found the right job. He had bumped into his old Captain accidentally. After that meeting the letter came offering him a job in Ireland. Peace-time in London was uneasy for Eden, the kind of job he looked for was scarce. Whole areas of the city were demolished. He was at a loss to find anyone who might help. It was good to renew old times in the army with Bradwell. The letter following the meeting was a surprise.

'I don't promise you anything definite but there may be a job here for you. The Grange has been empty during the war years. Now I need an overseer for the farm, whose duties would include staff management and general duties. The hours would be flexible and the work varied. Come and see. Stay as long as you wish. Yours, Bradwell.'

The offer seemed Godsent. He had accepted with speed and high hopes. Overseer on an Irish estate, steward of a stately home, agent, administrator, bailiff, he would cheerfully be any or all of these. He would do anything he was asked to get out of London. He'd had enough of city life.

He had no qualms, he was quick on the uptake, unafraid of work, prepared to learn any skill. He wrote that he would come immediately.

He had told Bradwell that he'd worked in insurance, that he'd like something less sedentary now. He would welcome responsibility and challenge. He must have impressed Brad. He also sensed that Brad missed the army. Hitler's antics had changed many lives, war rendered them topsy-turvy; it was hard to settle to peace again.

As far as Eden was concerned, he didn't fancy being ordered like a lackey any more. Having been commissioned, he'd a taste for authority; he didn't want desk work, he wanted power.

In actual fact he had never worked in an office or even owned a bank account until he joined the army. He had turned his hand to anything, been jack-of-all-trades in his time. He liked jobs to do with money, handling cash, putting it to better use. He had worked for a firm supplying penny-in-slot machines to pubs and arcades. Eden had emptied them, keeping tally of the cash. For a short time he had been a meter collector for the gas company. He had spent a long time on the Stoke Newington to Hammersmith bus route as a conductor, counting his takings with accuracy and speed. Making figures balance on paper was a joy and pride to him. Give him a column to tot and he didn't complain. He was above working on the buses now, having been an officer; he had experienced a better way of life. He could find nothing to suit him in London. Ireland was the answer. Ireland would bring him luck.

He had been curious about Bradwell's marriage to a widow with three daughters of her own. Since their marriage a son had been born. He had heard that the girls were good-looking and gifted. He looked forward to meeting them as much as he looked forward to a stately home. Landed gentry in Ireland were famed for comfortable living. Life in London was bomb damaged and depressing. A change would restore his soul.

There would be formal gardens, lawns shaded by yew trees. There would be greenhouses for rare blooms and fruit. Away from the mansion would be stables for horses and cattle, henhouses for the poultry, walled gardens for vegetables and more humble fruit. Figs on sunny walls, tennis courts, fountains awaited him. He would learn to fit in to high life, in the land of singing. Shamrocks would wave in the breeze.

Very likely he'd be put in charge of the accounts, he would handle the staff wages and check the invoices. From his office he would settle disputes with tradesmen who relied on the local gentry for their living.

Conditions might be difficult to start with, Brad having been away for so long. He, Eden, would restore the Grange to its former glory. He didn't expect to eat with the family each day, he'd have his own quarters over a garage or in an annexe, he wasn't fussy. A butler or housekeeper would bring him trays. Irish landowners were famed for their tables, the food would be supreme as well as the wine cellars. He was almost thirty, time to put down some roots. Where better than in the county of Armagh? He had health, quick wits, energy, he might even acquire an Irish wife.

He would wait until he had settled before stocking his wardrobe. He would see what was needed first. No doubt the list would include tweeds, jodhpurs and a hunting jacket (he disliked the idea of animal slaughter, loathed violence of any kind). Fishing tackle would be provided, very likely, as well as guns. He'd want a dinner jacket. The list seemed huge. Clothes bought locally would be cheaper and probably better cut. He had made inroads into his army gratuity, but he had a cheque book and no family ties.

He booked his ticket, via Liverpool, to Belfast on the *Ulster Monarch*. Life looked rich and wonderful. Work lay ahead in the country of colleens.

TWO

The taxi driver refused to drive him through the main gates, a small set-back and an indication of what lay ahead. The paint peeling from the gate posts was another sign. One gate was off its hinges, lying propped against the bank where it looked rather charming, with wild flowers pushing through the struts. Buttercups and dandelions tangled with a mauve flower that he thought was called vetch. Fuchsia flowers bloomed in the hedges. He paid the driver, who had barely spoken, he took his case and started to walk.

It was hot. The curving drive was bordered by horse-chestnut trees. He couldn't blame the driver for refusing to go further, the ground was pitted with potholes and what looked like cartwheel tracks. On his left was a disused cottage, probably a gardener's lodge once. Now a wild rose straggled round the door which opened in two halves like a stable . . . The windows were without glass. Piles of rubbish lay round it.

He enjoyed the walk, in spite of the heat. The mud of the drive gave off clouds of dust, making the weeds and grass each side look grey. It was mid-summer, there had been no rain for weeks.

The taxi man had been silent about Bradwell and his family. It was obvious now that the Grange wouldn't be grand at all. But he'd been invited, he was needed. Obviously there was work here, but not the kind he'd imagined.

The fields each side of the drive were empty, except for one boney cow. Far in the distance a donkey brayed. Clouds of flies buzzed round his head. More buzzed round the cow's head and tail. The swish of the tail, the cropping cow's jaws and the far-away donkey were peaceful sounds. The cow's nostrils were pink and wet. Eden didn't mind the heat, though he sweated heavily. He was in the country, with cows, flies, dust and dandelions. He'd meet Brad's family soon.

He paused by a clump of laurel bushes behind which lay the Grange and the lawns. He heard the singing before he saw them. He stood behind the bushes where they couldn't see him, peering through the leaves. He saw Bonnie first and his heart was lost. He knew that, no matter what the cost, he must stay.

There were two lawns, an upper and a lower, sloping down from the house, with steps to connect them. Bonnie was trying to wheel her little brother down the broken steps in a doll's pram: the boy was thin with longish hair. His legs hung over the pram wheels, he trailed his sandals in the grass. He had sticking plasters on his limbs and was sucking a grass stalk. The middle sister had a bowl of soapsuds; she sat on the steps blowing bubbles through a clay pipe. The third sister wasn't there.

They seemed heedless of anything but themselves and their bubble world. Their's seemed a magic capsule which he longed to enter. They looked invulnerable. The house behind was derelict and much smaller than he'd imagined. Tiles were missing from the roof, damp patches lay like blots on the walls, windows were boarded up. Ivy growing round the front door had loosened the pointing, the door itself looked rotten. There were no well-tended paths, no flowers or rose bushes, the two lawns were more like fields. He didn't mind; he'd seen Bonnie, lovelier than any flower. He listened.

'I'm forever blowing bubbles, pretty bubbles in the air. They fly so high, nearly reach the sky, then like my dreams they fade and die. Fortune's ever hiding, I search everywhere, I'm forever blowing bubbles, pretty bubbles in the air.' Bonnie's voice wasn't beautiful, more like a croak, but her beauty enchanted him.

The boy beat time languidly with his grass stalk. Bonnie half turned. Had she seen him? He stepped back, he mustn't interrupt their magic moment. He wanted to watch them for hours. She bumped the pram down, reaching to burst a bubble, her small breasts showing through her shirt. Her thighs were bare, all three wore shorts and old sandals. She went on reaching with her pretty hands. Was she doing it for him? Did she know her buttons were undone? He liked thin girls. In spite of her lovely smile she had an air of sorrow.

He cleared his throat. The boy spoke. 'Bonnie, someone is there.'

She started dramatically, moving a little towards the laurels, not looking at him. Then she buttoned her shirt.

She said loudly that the rubbish dump was the place for him. She pushed him onto a pile of weeds and grass cuttings.

'Sister, darling, you'll pay for that. You'll pay with your life.'

He was a handsome boy of about seven with a rather ratlike face. He lay and kicked his heels.

'A man is watching you, Bonnie. Look.'

She walked over to Eden, holding out her hand. 'Hullo, you must be Captain's friend. I'm Bonnie.'

Her speaking voice was beautiful, in contrast to when

she sang. The way she referred to her stepfather by rank seemed delightful. He'd been disappointed that no one had met him in the town, but he was getting his welcome now. Her hand was petal soft. He wondered where the parents were.

'Mamma is . . . busy, I'm afraid. Did you come in the town taxi?'

Tor, the younger sister, came over, the quieter one. The three of them were like figures in a play against the gloomy building behind. He didn't care if they were rich or poor, they had class, theirs was the world he wanted. Tor was thin, with cropped hair and narrower eyes than Bonnie's, less brilliant. She wasn't very much taller than the boy, still by the grass cuttings, waving his heels in the air.

He took Tor's hot hand. She smelled of fresh perspiration, like dandelion juice, not unpleasant. She didn't speak. She had a piercing gaze.

Bonnie was the hostess in her mother's absence. Had he had a pleasant trip? What time had he left London? He basked in the light of her smile. His life was changing. Birth and breeding surmounted poverty. A family tree cast a long shadow; doubtless theirs went back hundreds of years. He explained that he'd travelled on the mail boat.

The boy examined the sticking plaster on his knee. His limbs were scratched and scabbed. He gave his curiously rodent smile and asked if the sea had been rough.

'Stop asking questions. Get up, Bo.'

Bonnie said that her brother Boris was too inquisitive. The name Tor was short for Hortense. Ula, the youngest sister, was still in England, in hospital.

'Nothing serious, I hope?'

Bo told him that she had polio, the poor creature, had been flat on her back for months. He spoke with a fluctuating brogue but his sisters spoke with the kind of purity that Eden most admired, that you heard on the BBC. He told them he'd enjoyed his trip and was delighted to see Ireland at last.

In fact he'd been up in the bar all night, listening to the other travellers celebrating their return home. He wanted to save buying a berth. He had drunk almost nothing, but was exhausted now. Nothing so far had turned out as he'd expected, but he didn't regret coming. There was work here, he would be needed. There was Bonnie. He would make sure that these kids needed him. Yes, he'd enjoyed the trip.

'You served under my father, didn't you? Did you kill anyone? Did you like the war?'

Eden explained to Bo that he'd been in Tunisia with Bradwell for a short time. War was not something to enjoy, you made the best of it. War caused disruption, if not catastrophe. Death was not something to glorify.

He had a horror of bloodshed or rage of any kind, but he had enjoyed the war. It had opened his eyes to another way of life, he had met new people from new backgrounds. He liked order, the mindless drilling on parade grounds; the cleaning and polishing were good discipline. As an eventual motor transport driver for officers, he'd become ambitious. Finally, he'd become an officer himself. His acceptance into the Officers' Training Unit was a landmark. He would never return to his old way of life or mix with his old companions. The pip on his shoulder gave him a new pride and opened new doors. He had done everything to the best of his ability, but patriotism, the war effort, defeating Hitler, held no interest for him. His own self-improvement counted more. His uniform flattered him, an officer had an active social life. He'd been sorry when the war had stopped.

Meeting Bradwell again was a stroke of luck. He was here, the sky was the limit now.

Bo lay on the grass still, his hair fanned over a patch of

clover. He stared up with light-coloured eyes. He'd like to be an army band master. He wouldn't mind being the Pope.

'You look like a casualty of war,' Eden said, pointing to the sticking plasters.

Bo pointed two fingers at them. 'Bang-bang. You're dead. How old are you?'

'Stop it, Bo,' Bonnie said.

'I'm only after asking because of Dadda needing someone young to help.' Bo reached for the soap bowl, blowing into it through his grass stalk, making the foam rise.

'Where is your father?'

'He'll be in soon. Mamma . . . is . . . lying down,' Bonnie said.

'Not ill, I hope? The heat . . .'

Bo said that his Mammy lay down in her room often. The one he missed most was Ula, poor creature.

'Well, she's not here. You must make do with Tor and me.'

'Sisters three, ah me, ah me,' Bo sighed poetically.

Tor leaned over him. Ula would write to him soon.

He blew another mournful blast down his grass stalk. The women in his life were suffocating, he said. He wanted to go to the Christian Brothers' school.

They left the pram on the lawn and went in.

Lunch was eaten in the kitchen, overlooking the stable yard at the back. The long pine table, the copper pans on the wall, the heavy plate racks were evidence of past wealth, but now the table had a broken leg, the pans had holes, there were no plates in the racks. Some of the floor tiles were cracked or missing; a fern forced its way up near the sink. There was a smell of sour milk and must. Eden noticed these details with pleasure; the more neglect there was, the more work for him both inside and outside the Grange. The light bulb flickered. It was pleasantly cool and dim.

He went on observing and listening as they sat round the table. The torn napkins, the miserable utensils and cutlery confirmed the truth; Bradwell had hit on hard times, was very likely in dire straits. Why didn't he appear? Where was the mother? She'd been resting now for hours. The kids seemed very much alone. He mustn't stare so much at Bonnie. Lunch, made by Tor on an ancient range, was a sort of soup of potatoes and milk; he had to force it down. There was an open fireplace that needed cleaning. Each time Bonnie opened her mouth for her spoon he glimpsed her sweet pink tongue and his longings started.

A duck waddled across the back doorstep, its eyes were a cold, unfriendly black. At least they had some poultry as well as one thin cow. Bo jumped up and snatched his duck. It was his pet, his lucky duck. The bird flapped and squawked, freeing itself. In the yard was a gulley with a trickle of water, the duck retreated into the heat again.

Bo was responsible for the egg collection. His duck might lay anywhere.

'Only one duck?'

'We did have another. It died.'

Sometimes the eggs smelled, having lain undiscovered for weeks. Ducks made good mothers, Bo said, being more intelligent than hens. Their eggs tasted oily. He waved his spoon about as he gave this information. Would Eden like to help him look for eggs? His careless little birdeen sometimes laid indoors.

Eden was still wondering about their mother. Shouldn't they take her some lunch? It was all so quiet.

Old dung lay round the yard. The door at the end of the barn led to the back field. No kitchen gardens, no greenhouses or fountains, just one duck and one thin cow.

But when he was in charge, he told himself, it would all change; the Grange would prosper again. They found an egg in a patch of thistles. Bo wiped it clean, smelling it. Rotten, as he'd feared. Ah me.

Eden was already starting a mental list of requirements. That yard was insanitary; they'd need brooms, shovels, a proper wheelbarrow. He would need building materials. He would need to learn about crop rotation and the rudiments of poultry keeping. He would forget grandiose ideas. That barn looked reasonably weathertight. The house needed rewiring, the damp parts cut out and restored. There was enough here to keep him busy for years ahead. He'd wanted a change, wanted challenge. Here it was.

'Bo, exactly where is your father? It's getting late.'

Bo blinked, he put his hand in Eden's. The boy's hand was sticky, he felt the sticking plaster against his wrist. Was he accident prone? He mustn't upset him. Why did he speak with that brogue?

The state of the rooms upstairs was what you'd expect. The bathroom had to be seen to be believed. The vast iron bath on claw feet, the tangle of piping, the rusted geyser, were from another age. On the window sill was a huge artificial rose. Someone had spilled tooth powder.

Eden had the room next to the girls' room at the top of the stairs. There were no carpets on the unpolished boards. Bo had the tiny room by the bathroom. There was one attic room on the top floor, the domain of his host and hostess. He still hadn't seen or heard them by night time.

Eden pressed himself against the wall that separated him from the two girls. He heard one of them laugh. No one had laughed downstairs. Were they talking about him? He went over the bubble song in his mind.

THREE

A mosquito hummed by the window, then by his bed, annoyingly close to his head. He grabbed at it, there was silence. Then it started again. It was too hot for pyjamas, even the air was too much on his skin.

He had pulled his bed under his window to overhear what the sisters said. Outside he could make out the laurel bushes, a lumpy shape in the dark. Was Brad even in this country? Did they have a mother at all?

He'd not liked to keep asking questions, there'd been no sound from the attic overhead. These kids were too young to be left alone; though Bonnie wasn't a child she was defenceless.

He pushed his sheets onto the floor. He liked a firm mattress, not a lumpy one; this one was what you'd expect. He stared out again. A thin moon showed from behind a cloud. He was moon-struck over Bonnie, he must reach up to his goddess, make her his own.

He couldn't sleep for thinking about her. There was no sound now from next door. Were her eyes like forget-me-nots or hyacinths? Her hair was so silky, her infrequent smile so sad. She'd made a brave effort to welcome him, she'd been a mother to her little brother; putting him to bed, putting fresh plasters on his scabs, washing him, singing in that odd, growling way, almost one note. She must be tone-deaf, that wouldn't change. Bo liked being petted, insisting on being sung to sleep.

He mused over the events of the day. The Grange was a fiasco, this country a let-down, but he'd found her, all else faded.

His bedroom had only a bed, a chair and an old-fashioned washstand. Someone had put a branch of hawthorn in a jamjar on the marble top, it had bitter-smelling blooms. Had Bonnie put them there? Beautiful Bonnie of the luminous eyes was next door to him, sleeping the sleep of innocence.

He'd found a bulb for the kitchen light but the flex was damaged. Most of the switches were corroded, he'd got a mild shock off one.

Those eyes were familiar, he'd seen them somewhere, he couldn't place her. Had she travelled on his bus years ago? He had a long memory for faces, hers was elusive. He'd made a habit of listening and watching all his life; his method of self-improvement.

If he had a weakness, it was a hatred of reading; he never read a book or even a newspaper if he could avoid it. Reading was time-consuming and tiresome, a retentive mind was as good as the printed word. He'd been forced to study at the Officers' Training Unit; since that time he'd lived by his wits, listening, practising, copying.

He was particular about cleanliness, the state of this house came as a shock. He'd be needed, that was what mattered. He'd even take to reading if Bonnie wished.

As a child he had lived with his aunt in Streatham; they had not been happy years. He had loathed his time at school. His real education didn't start until he'd left Streatham and put Aunt from his mind.

As he lay in the heat thinking of Bonnie, he remembered something that happened with his aunt. He'd been about eleven, wearing a pair of new long trousers, sitting at the table waiting for tea. Somehow the plate had been knocked from Aunt's hand as she was putting it in front of him, his new trousers had been spoiled. He had watched scrambled egg trickling down his fly buttons, along his thighs and into his shoes. Aunt's anger had been more upsetting than egg in his buttonholes. She had dabbed her cloth at him. Nasty little boy, had he no idea of decency? Dab-dab. Look at the state of him, did he think new trousers grew on trees? Couldn't he control himself? Dab-dab, dirty brat. She'd never asked to have him, didn't need or deserve him. Dab-dab. He was nothing but extra work.

He had run upstairs to get away from her, had stood by his bed holding himself until misery turned to comfort, his body eased. He glowed with warmth, he clutched harder, his jet spurted, again, again. Forget Aunt, let it go, release it. Yes. Over the blanket, over his trousers, egg and sperm in a widening stream. He mopped at it, breath panting. Aunt mustn't see, mustn't know about it. She would kill him if she knew.

They had shared nothing but the roof, he'd never confided in her. When he got bullied at school, he'd not told. The boys sniffed and sniggered, boys with parents and noisy homes. You became secretive early, you survived by cunning, you learned to imitate and to lie. He'd made a point of keeping quiet and neat, of making no mess, and keeping out of Aunt's way. Was she a real aunt or a foster parent? Mustn't be a nuisance, mustn't ask questions, so he never knew. What mattered was learning to please. His anxieties over his sexual development must be ignored. The down on his upper lip, his body hair, his voice that squeaked up and down must be ignored. Don't question, don't draw attention to yourself. Listen and watch, bide your time.

The egg episode was a small landmark, but by the time war broke out Streatham was a memory. By then he was on his way up in the world, he'd never gone back, never written, hardly thought of her. She used to fix him with her small eyes, her damp grey lips and given this advice: 'Be content with your lot. Ambition killed the rat.'

He was destined to climb, he'd known it for years. At fifteen he was on his own. Though he'd never lost his feeling of loneliness, he'd grown used to it. He had set himself to learn what and what not to do. He'd learned how to make girls interested, using flattery and kindness, had learned how to make them say yes. Not being tall, he naturally preferred small slender girls. He'd found a room in Clerkenwell and settled to improving himself.

At first he had joined a boys' club. He'd learned wrestling, then, more importantly, he'd learned ballroom dancing. Dancing became a passion as well as an opportunity to socialize. His first real girlfriend had been thirteen, but looked older, with a foxy face, thin lips and ginger hair. He had taught her to tango; later, when jiving swept the dance halls, they'd been champions. Together they studied pornographic magazines, knew where blue movies could be seen, and had been happy. She'd needed no teaching in bed. It came naturally, whether dancing or making love. When the war started he'd joined up and moved away. She'd been young enough to be evacuated to the country. They had vowed fidelity, the war kept them apart. Neither were keen letter writers; sometimes he regretted leaving school early, but hating books as he did, he'd had no choice. He became a student of life, with three interests; wrestling, ballroom dancing and making love. These interests narrowed to sex and dancing. He took up simple book-keeping instead of wrestling. He seemed to have been acquiring knowledge all his life. To please his aunt he'd learned housework in Streatham, had shopped, washed dishes and cleaned. He brought tea to her bedside each morning, he cleaned and lit her kitchen fire before leaving for school.

His fires were a source of pride to him. First you raked the ashes, setting aside any clinkers to lay each side of the grate. Newspaper must be crumpled loosely under the kindling wood, the layer of fresh, small coal pieces was the finishing touch. Aunt would come down, see the blaze but never thank or praise him.

He hated her, she resented him. The egg episode strengthened his resolve to leave when he was old enough. He'd acquired patience and a few basic skills in Streatham.

When he was called up he'd left his job on the 73 bus route, said goodbye to his red-headed girl friend and started to climb further in the world. At the end of his service his sights were set, his ambition crystallized, he would be middle class in future, Streatham and Clerkenwell didn't exist. He would look different, he would speak correctly, paying attention to each inflection, each vowel sound. He would be assured and easy in all situations, would bask in affluence and leisure. He never wanted to see a bedsitter again. He never wanted to open a rent book or put money in a slot meter or deal with a landlady. He was through with cheap dance halls and cheap girls. He would be quiet and moderate in all things. The army had taught him to hold his cutlery correctly, to move in a measured way, to open doors for ladies and the elderly, to give orders firmly when the occasion arose. He had little money and few specialized skills, he had boundless ambition, he was a power-house of energy.

He'd been working particularly hard on his vowel sounds when he'd bumped into Brad in Piccadilly. His greeting, 'Hey I know you. I remember you,' had been faultless. Brad's invitation was his reward. His appearance had altered as well as his speech and behaviour. Gone were the crooked teeth, the slicked and greasy hair of the army days. With straightened teeth, expensive barbering and small moustache he was another person. His eyebrows were thinned, his nails manicured, he sometimes smoked a cigar. A daily bath was something he took for granted now, the hint of grey at his temples was just right. He was a fitting recipient for the invitation to Ireland.

The poverty he'd found here didn't dismay him. Nothing overruled breeding and class.

He lay pondering in the stifling room. He must be consistent, reliable and calm. He repeated a little rhyme he'd invented for his vowel sounds: 'Brown frowned on his way down town. He must save to pay Jane's way.' His stomach rattled, he'd eaten almost nothing all day. At least his aunt had fed him, he could say that for her. Not like these kids. He felt clothed all over in damp. He stroked himself slowly, with finesse, to induce sleep, climaxing without intention, warm spouts over his hand; and, in coming, he remembered. He *had* seen Bonnie before, years ago. She'd been at the posh boarding school in the West Country where his redhead had been evacuated for a short time. He had visited her for an illicit night. Yes, Bonnie had been one of the girls there. Little did he think that he'd ever be visiting one of those stuck-up kids, as an equal, as a guest. They were not entire strangers, though they'd not spoken and he, of course, had changed totally. He lay still, marvelling at fate.

He must get a hanky, mustn't mark the mattress; to leave stains would be ill-bred. It would dry, he could turn it over. He rolled up his hanky and put it in his case. He was starving. What kind of parents would leave these kids without food?

He made further plans as he drifted to sleep. He would start in the kitchen; they must have proper light, though he'd had little electrical experience. He'd be their benefactor.

The morning was dull and sunless, very likely they'd

have storms. He washed and shaved in the terrible bathroom, not liking to risk the geyser. He trimmed his moustache, rolled up his sleeves and went down.

Tor was eating porridge by the stove, holding her bowl in her hand. Bonnie was sitting by the window with a mirror balanced against the sill. She was combing her hair over her face, covering it. She wore a pyjama top over her shorts, she was examining the tips of her hair. Bleached gold from sun and wind, it shaded darker at the roots. It *was* the same girl he'd glimpsed briefly all those years ago, he was sure of it. You couldn't forget those eyes. She looked at him through the darker and light-coloured hair, so piercingly blue, so luminous, eyes that a man could die for.

'Porridge, Eden?' Tor had cooked a lot.

'I haven't eaten that since I was a lad . . . a boy, I mean.'

Eating at breakfast was something he'd given up years back. Black coffee and fruit juice were more high class; the days of toast with marge and mugs of tea in Streatham were gone. He took a little porridge, struggling to swallow the lumps and leathery skin. The milk in the jug was sour. Tor wore a sacking apron that nearly touched the floor, her expression was stern. None of them wore shoes. Bo's hair was still tangled with grass and burrs. He had a letter.

'Your postman must come early,' Eden said, forcing another spoonful down. The letter was from Ula. Bo read it in a loud, self-conscious voice. 'Ask Mamma to find a hospital in Ireland. It's awful here . . . Please ask.'

'Poor little girl. You must be worried about her. Where is your mother, actually? Is she better?'

Tor swilled cold water over her porridge bowl. Bonnie still combed her hair over her face.

'Tor, where are your parents? Are they here at all?'

'It isn't that . . .'

'What did you say? Look at me, Bonnie. Where is Bradwell? Where is your mother?'

She threw down her comb and went out, her bare feet making no sound on the stairs. She had such beautiful long legs, such delicate skin behind the knees, he had to follow her. He'd upset her, he hadn't meant it, he half stumbled over a loose board. Missing planks, rot and fungus, what a setting for such a girl. The door of their room was open; there she was, on the bed.

'Don't run away, Bonnie. I want to help. What is it? Please?'

She was by the window, her head in her hands, rocking herself. She needed comforting; he would be bold, he would sit down by her. This mattress was even thinner than his, he felt her fine hair and her ear by his cheek. Her neck drooped so touchingly, he would let her cry, patting her gently. All three of them were much too thin. He could smell cheap shampoo in this room as well as mould.

'It's Mamma, you see. We're worried. Well, not worried exactly, just concerned. Did you guess?'

'I did wonder. She's not here, is she?'

'She's not in her room, she's not at home.'

'And Brad? What about your father?'

'He's gone too. He often does. He goes drinking and upsets Mamma.'

He told her to try not to worry about them. He was here and he would help.

FOUR

He wasn't completely surprised, he had half guessed. No one was dead, it was simply a domestic upset. It was his chance to get down to practicalities, curb his urge to gaze at Bonnie's pale breasts. He must concentrate on all three; Bo's scratches looked nasty, he might need medical care. They all needed properly feeding; they didn't seem properly clothed. Bonnie's hair was warm, like greased feathers near his cheek. He looked into her eyes. Do not fear. I am here to help.

'A drinking father isn't so terrible. Try not to worry so much.'

Her real father had been dead a long time. Very likely she'd expected Brad to be a demi-god, to compensate for what she'd lost. Family circles were rarely perfect. Certainly this one was not. Brad hadn't been a heavy drinker in the army days. Very likely he was still adjusting to civvy street and a ready-made family. He must have been shocked at the deterioration of the Grange and the daunting repairs he faced. He might be missing the army responsibilities. No troops to command now, just a wife and kids stuck in a dull, quiet place. The wife complained, Eden imagined. He'd find out in due course.

All his previous ideas had proved false. The family were depressed, the house a disgrace. He'd come in the nick of time.

Tor and Bo had followed him upstairs. Bo watched him with his goat-like stare that reminded Eden of Brad.

'I'll find your father,' he told them. 'Don't worry anymore.'

'We aren't worried, just a bit concerned. Mamma . . .'

'Do you know where she went?'

'She gets so miserable. She doesn't always leave . . .'

'Once she went to a hotel,' Bo said sharply.

'And left you alone?'

'We're not neglected. Don't imagine we are.'

Tor was proud, to pity them was insulting. She came to the bed and sat on Bonnie's other side. Bo followed, he looked flushed. Eden told them it would all blow over. Privately he was outraged. He would start a search party right away, the drunken head of the family must be restored. Bo could come too if he liked, and his sisters.

The girls decided to stay at home in case their mother returned. Bo would go with Eden to the town.

The sole of Bo's sandal flapped in the dirt as the two set off along the drive. He still had burrs in his hair. It was gloomy now under the chestnut trees, the leaves hung slack in the heavy heat. The girls had taken the cow to the barn for milking. There was a smell of dung and flying ants swarmed in the air. Bo made little rushes at them, lashing them with a blade of grass. Except for the bubble pipe, he seemed to have no playthings. They might find some comics in the town, or a water-pistol.

'If you see a duck around, let me know,' Bo said. He had two once, but one had gone, eaten perhaps by a fox. Ducks survived better than hens.

'Who lived here before, Bo?'

'No one. We were in England. Dadda was an officer in the war.'

'I know that. I was there. He offered me a job.'

'I'm here to help him. I'm my Da's right-hand man. We can manage.'

'Wouldn't you like me to stay?'

'We can manage, I said.'

His brogue fluctuated. Did he speak like that to gain confidence? Eden cut him a switch, stripping the leaves back, leaving two at the end as a weapon against the ants. A wasp loomed near. Take care, Eden told him, insect bites at this time of year could turn septic. Bo was scratched and scarred enough. Could he have been assaulted or was he accident prone? Nothing would surprise Eden now. Meanwhile, Brad must be found.

There were the white gates again, one propped against the bank, the other half falling from one hinge. There was the gardener's lodge even seedier looking now, in the dull morning light. Drops of rain started falling as they went onto the road. In the distance the donkey brayed again.

Bo said the storm would start in half an hour, he was used to forecasting the weather. He loved Ireland, one day he'd run the Grange. Eden tried to picture it in fifteen years' time with Bo, a strapping young man, and herds of cattle, while Bonnie and her sister skimmed cream and churned butter pats. The picture was unlikely, he didn't want a milkmaid for a wife. He himself knew little about animal husbandry or even the behaviour of cows, bulls and calves. He didn't like to ask Bo. It seemed their neighbours had a bull when they needed one, their cow hadn't calved for a long time. To Eden, the cow seemed dangerously thin.

'I wouldn't mind finding my drake. I saw a stuffed duckling once, all fluffy and yellow. My sisters hate that cow.'

'You are fond of your sisters, aren't you?'

'They have their uses. They need me for their silly games.'

'But you like living here?'

'I do, of course, I'm Irish. Those creatures have no Irish blood. Not like me and Dadda.'

'And your mother? How does she feel?'

'She doesn't belong. No one understands.'

'Understands what?'

The boy said that he didn't worry about his father. He would be in Fagin's Bar.

The rain became heavier, falling straight from the sky on them. The hawthorn in the hedges was pungent. Eden had no jacket with him, the rain felt almost warm. What a good thing he'd spared himself the expense of new clothes, all he'd need for the time being were wellingtons, cords and some sandals for relaxing in, like the ones these kids wore. If, indeed, he'd find time to relax. A magpie hopped before them. Bo said that the old rhyme about one magpie meaning sorrow wasn't true. The magpie was the sorry one, because of having no mate.

Eden asked about his school. When would he start?

'It's not arranged. I want to go to the Christian Brothers'. They teach woodwork and farm management.'

Eden hadn't thought of Bradwell as being Roman Catholic. Did he go to Mass?

Bo answered indignantly. He and his Da were proper Irishmen, not like his mother and those girls. The Brothers had a special bus for the children. He'd be picked up at the end of the drive. His mammy wanted him to go to an English boarding school. He *must* go to a Catholic school, because he might be a priest one day. He wrote verses, that was his hobby, he didn't miss England at all. His mammy didn't like it here; his sisters, poor old creatures, didn't know what they *did* want. As he spoke, the boy lashed his switch at the rain.

A collie dog met them at the town's main street, which was wide, with low grey houses each side, a few shops and some pubs. At the far end was a garage with two petrol pumps and a pub called Fagin Bros. The sign over the door was painted boldly in gold lettering. The church was half a mile further on, there was a sawmill too, Bo said. Eden wondered why it should be called a town; it was a hamlet, depressingly empty and quiet. The rain beat on the pavements, spattering the canvas sunblinds covering front doors. The double doors of the Co-op stores were shut. A notice said 'Back at half three.' The windows on either side were stacked with boxes of soap flakes and scouring powder. A blue enamel washing bowl said 'Washday made Bright'. In spite of the rain you could smell the petrol dripping from the petrol pump opposite Fagin Bros. The collie hung its tongue as if to catch the rain. Fagin's was closed too.

Eden looked over the top of the brass rail that held the red curtains across the window. There was Brad with his back to him, half lying along the bar. He saw the barman coming from the back with a drink in his hand, he had a cruel look on his face. Brad took the whisky, gulped it and reached for his beer. Alternating beer with spirits was a quick way to oblivion, Eden hadn't expected it of Brad. He was wearing the same clothes he'd worn when they'd met in London. Now they looked as if he'd slept in them. His brogues were stained, a slug or snail seemed to have left tracks across his shoulders; buttons were gone, his hands unwashed.

'I'll go first, Eden. Stay.'

Bo pushed the door, his sandal flapped on the step. He touched Brad with his wet chestnut switch.

'I'm here now, Dadda. Come on home.'

Brad turned. He looked at his son with unfocused eyes.

'Has she . . . did . . . she?'

'She didn't come back yet. Come on, Da.'

Brad went on staring. His mouth was slack, the pupils of his eyes were small. He had the distant look of a homeless person, beyond sorrow.

The collie rested under a table, the marble top made it cool and dark.

'A big storm is coming, Dadda. Eden arrived. See?'

'Eden? You? Here? You're early. How are you? You're a day early.'

'I came yesterday. We arranged for yesterday, Brad. Remember?'

'No matter. You're here. You're welcome. Have a drink.'

FIVE

'There's a storm brewing up. We should go back now.'
   'Back? What storm? Have a drink. There's no storm.'
   'Another time, Brad. With pleasure. Let's go now.'
   As Eden spoke, sheet lightning lit the street. 'Washday made Bright' shone in glory, the brass rail in the window shone like gold. Thunder drowned Bo's voice as he pulled his father's sleeve. Another flash lit the brass letter-flap of the Co-op and the petrol pumps. There were no other people in sight. Bo had said that his father often met the bank manager on the days that he came back drunk. Eden couldn't see a bank or a post office, perhaps they were further on, near the church. Rain washed the petrol drips from the garage forecourt.
   'There's no storm. Forget the storm. Have a drink.'
   'Come home now, Dadda.'
   Straight-falling, hard rain had turned the street into a sheet of water almost level with Fagin's step.
   'Come, Dadda.'
   Outside in the rain Brad was docile, his hand was light and damp on Eden's wrist. They walked slowly, Bo was a step behind in case his father swayed. Brad kept his eyes

half closed. Their clothes soon felt like tight skins that stuck to them. Except for the barman with the hostile eyes, no one saw them arrive or leave. Perhaps more eyes watched from behind curtains and blinds. Perhaps someone peeped from behind the basin claiming to make washday bright. Where was the garage owner, the Co-op assistant? Were there no teachers or priests in this town? The collie watched them leave from the step, the fur on its head and shoulders clotted with wet, then returned to the table. They didn't look back.

The hedges were flattened, beaten down with wet. The road stretched ahead, black and long. The rain thickened to hailstones, small and light, stinging their skins as they got larger. Eden led Brad by the hand. The only dry parts of him were the soles of his feet. Bo's bare toes gleamed through his sandal straps, his loose flap of sole had gone. Brad tripped. His face, washed of grease and sweat, looked as innocent as Bo's. He placed his feet delicately, straddling them, not noticing the storm; walking without falling took his attention. At last the Grange gates were in sight.

'Steady, Da. Nearly home.'

Bradwell pulled free from Eden and leaned over the broken gate. Drink exhausted you as well as robbing your wits. His hair fell forward like quills as he leaned over the gate. He belched. A stream of saliva followed by vomit poured from his mouth. A clap of thunder broke over their heads. Bo stood by his father, tight-faced. The flowers in the grass under the gate were covered with vomit.

'Come, Dadda. Nearly home.'

Vomit dripped from Brad's chin, glittering. Carroty shreds shone in the pale buff, soaking the roots of the buttercups. His feet slipped, he grasped at Bo, ignoring Eden's hand. He muttered.

'Brad-well, you are a disaster. You've let the family down. Dis-aster. Dis-grace.'

Eden took his shoulders.

'Come on. Don't give way. Don't give way now. Let's shelter here in the lodge.'

They steered him through the gap in the wall and over the pile of masonry and tin cans in front of the door. It wasn't locked. The one room inside was dry, bare and clean. It opened into a lean-to shed where a tap dripped into a bucket. In the corner a ladder led to a loft. The windows on each side of the door were without glass, the overhanging eaves kept the room dry. In the hearth were the charred remains of a log fire. Bo kicked at a cinder. Ash flew.

'Someone must have been here,' Eden said. It didn't feel disused. It was a good shelter. Had anyone lived here recently?

'It's not used. It's never used. It hasn't been lived in for years.'

Brad didn't speak. He went to the mantelpiece, gripping it with dirty fingers. The air began to stink of drink.

'Look, Dadda, it's getting light. The rain is stopping. Look. Light.'

Bo leaned through a window with his hand out. It was dark still but the thunder had ceased.

'A disaster,' Brad muttered again.

The rain drummed on the tin roof of the outhouse.

'Come, Dadda. Let's go.'

Brad lifted his head from the mantelpiece.

'Come here, you little brat. I want you.'

'Brad, he's only anxious to get back to his sisters. They'll be worrying.'

'Stay out of it, you. It's not your business. Come here, Bo. Who has been here? Has *she*? . . . Answer me, you brat.'

'Of course not. No one has. The rain is stopping. It's gone.'

'Don't, Bradwell. Let the boy alone.'

'What's it to you? I know your game, Eden. I have no ill-usions, no ill-usions at all.'

'What do you mean, Brad?'

'What? I will tell you, I will elu-cidate. You are trying to make yourself indis . . . indis . . . indispensable. I know your game.'

'You are wrong, sir. I'm doing no such thing.'

'No? "No such thing"? I know your sort. You'll be setting your cap at my daughter next. Oh yes . . . Oh yes.'

'Don't be ridiculous, Brad. I only just arrived. You invited me, remember? You offered me the job.'

'Job? What job? There's no job here, can't you see? A dis-aster.'

'Don't, Dadda, don't be upset again.'

'Bo. My son. My son.'

Brad's mood changed to self-pity again. Hadn't he always done his best? Where had he gone wrong? He deserved better than this. Where was she? Why? Why?

'I'm here, Dadda. Don't be sad.'

'Son. Son.'

The two stood by the fireplace. Eden was excluded. He'd been condemned, the outsider with designs. Not needed. Not wanted here.

He left them. Let them follow or not as they pleased. He had done what he'd set out for, he had brought the runaway back. He must rejoin the daughters waiting behind without proper food or light.

A faint streak of yellow showed over the chestnut trees. The dust and flies were gone, now each leaf dripped. A bird cheeped. He wondered where the magpie was. Bonnie was his main concern, her well-being was all that mattered. He reached the bushes, the grass looked as if it had turned liquid. Rain washed down the steps over the upturned pram. He looked up and saw the girls leaning against their window pane. Rain blurred their faces. How long had they been waiting, heads close, arms entwined? He shouted up.

'We're back. Safe and sound. Bo and your dad are coming behind.'

They didn't wave or answer, staring and waiting. Behind him, Brad and Bo followed, making their slow way.

'Easy now, Da,' he heard Bo say. 'Take your time, Dadda, that's the way.'

Brad went to the lavatory leading from the hall. They heard the seat crash down before he sat down with a great sigh.

Bo waited outside, his face strained and tight still. He tried to smile. His dadda was all right. He was grand.

In the kitchen the remains of breakfast were still on the table. Eden filled the kettle. Bo said his father liked his tea strong.

'Should we check that he's all right? He's a long time there.'

Snores sounded from behind the lavatory door. His father got tired, Bo said. He'd a lot of worry. People didn't understand.

'I want to understand, Bo. I can't if no one explains.'

'It's not his fault. It isn't. It isn't.'

The girls were still in their bedrooms. Eden and Bo drank some tea. The Irish were a nation of tea drinkers, Eden remembered. What a lackadaisical family this was.

The lock was clicking, the door was opening. Brad came out.

'Bo? Where are you? C'm'ere, I want you. I'm going up.'

Eden came behind them. Getting him up the second flight was worst. The stairs twisted half way up, at the turn Brad missed a step, falling forward on his face. He lay filling the stairway, muttering in a surprised way. He'd let them down. A disaster, he admitted it. Where was she, anyway?

Bo pulled at his hands, Eden pushed and supported him, they reached the attic. Bradwell made for the bed.

To Eden's surprise, the room was inviting; no sign of

poverty anywhere. He had expected full ashtrays, dirty glasses, stains and torn sheets. The attic was peaceful and bright. Under the skylight was a brass bed heaped with cushions and silk-fringed shawls. There was a white fur rug as well as Persian carpets. The white walls had jade and rose quartz beads hanging from ornate brass hooks, echoing the greens and pinks of the rugs. A cane hamper spilled satin and silken clothing, there were shoes, scarves, flowery hats. The effect was artistic rather than slovenly. There was disorder but nothing cheap or soiled. He wondered if the mother had left halfway through packing her things. He saw a purse under the bed. Bo kicked it out of sight. The scent of rose perfume was sweet and heady. Brad pitched onto the bed and slept.

Eden felt the tension go out of Bo. Peace at last. His dad was safely back. Brad was the boy's responsibility, his sisters could worry about their mother; the Irish members of the family stuck close.

He lifted his father's feet, one by one; unlacing the shoes, he covered him with a shawl. His father must be left quiet and comfortable. He wrung out a flannel at the washstand, he tenderly wiped Brad's face. He put the china basin beside him in case of emergency. He must have a hot-water bottle. Later, he must have strong tea. Their two faces were more alike than ever, rat-sharp noses, wide-spaced eyes, a lost yet innocent air.

'Does he usually sleep for long, Bo?'

The boy said he would be unlikely to waken before morning. They could go down now, they could all relax.

Bonnie was doing her hair again in the kitchen, her face hidden. Tor was wiping the table in a worried way, her hand moving in circles. He longed to reassure them, to comfort and protect them. Bonnie's hand with her comb was shaking. She kept her eyes hidden behind her hair.

'He's asleep. He's quite all right now, no harm done.'

'It isn't him. It's Mamma.'

'What happened, Bonnie?'

The postman had brought a message from Fagin's farm, just before the storm broke. Their mother was there, she was coming home later.

Eden felt enraged. She had left three nervous kids with a drunken father while she went visiting. Didn't she have any sense of responsibility? Selfish bitch, thinking only of herself. No doubt she was afraid of Brad in that condition, no doubt she found life here a trial. She should have checked before she came to live here, the Irish were different. Irishmen drank to get drunk, drunkenness was accepted lightly. She should have checked up on the state of the Grange. No doubt she missed the parties and admiration she'd been used to, very likely she was a snob as well. If she was lonely, she'd brought it on herself. Her attic revealed a lot about her; her own room was attractive and comfortable, no matter about anywhere else. He remembered the way Bo had kicked the purse away. It wouldn't surprise him if the kid wasn't light-fingered. A lot was wrong with this family. A good thing he'd come when he had. At least they knew where the mother was, the bitch, the selfish snob. She'd be back when it suited her, doubtless.

'Poor Dadda must have a hot-water bottle,' Bo said.

'Poor Dadda nothing. He's drunk, and you know it. He's filthy and disgusting. And stop calling him Dadda. It's silly, it's stage-Irish. Can't you say "Captain" like we do? Can't you be natural?'

'He's my blood father, I'm not like you two. You're mongrels, you have no father. I have my Da . . . I love him and he loves me, I'll call him what I like. He's my friend.'

'Friend? Oh very friendly I must say, coming home in that state, time after time.'

Bickering seemed to give the kids relief, they seemed to

enjoy it. The immediate crisis was over, they could relax; scrapping eased tension. What they needed now was a proper meal. He would go now and buy groceries. Perhaps Bonnie would come with him.

But all three preferred to stay. The girls wanted to be here when their mother turned up; it was understandable. Bo had his father on his mind. Eden suggested lighting the range. They could have hot water then. He had never laid a turf fire before; the feel of the sods pleased him, dry and rough, the colour of cork. You laid them on end, round a wad of newspaper. When alight, they smelled like burning leaves, collapsing into orange-coloured ash.

He left the three of them warming themselves and throwing fresh turf into the grate. Though it was hot still, it was damp. The firelight cheered. As he left they started humming their bubble song very softly. Bonnie droned on one note. They were an odd lot, no doubt of that, but he was committed to them.

Another downpour looked imminent, after the lull in the storm. He was beginning to feel part of the place; the dripping trees, the drive, the sodden fields were familiar now. There was the thin cow, lashing its tail. The message on the Co-op door was still there, 'Back at half three'. The town was still empty, the barman in Fagin's still there. At the back of his bar was a small parlour stocked with groceries. Cornflakes, tea, eggs were on a shelf. There were tins of meat and peas. There were stools here where friends of the barman could drink in private. He was surly with Eden, wrapping the purchases without speaking, knotting them with string. Behind were dusty liqueur bottles as well as spirits. A bottle of crême de menthe looked years old. Did Brad buy drink to take home, or did he do all his serious drinking here?

'Very quiet, aren't we?' He planned to be here a long time, he might as well be friendly.

The man was silent, the collie dog slept. Where was the famous Irish bonhomie that he'd heard about? Except for that attic bedroom, everywhere had an air of heaviness and doom. Even Aunt's house in Streatham had some life compared to this place. How shocked she'd be to see it here. 'Be content with your lot. Ambition killed the rat.' He couldn't agree with that. Life had soured his aunt, it wouldn't sour him. Her grey night-time plait of hair, her teeth in the tumbler, her mustard paintwork, were things to be forgotten. He would change everything that he could change. Poor little Bonnie must be rescued. She needed clothes, a proper diet, someone to care.

He had left her holding a towel to the fire for her bath later. Her toes had looked so pretty and pink. They were still sitting there when he got back.

'We'll have a good fry-up, shall we? I got sausages. How about some chips?'

Before they ate they stacked the turf baskets high with turf from the turf shed. They pulled chairs round the fire, they talked with their mouths full, spearing chips and pieces of sausage onto their knives, eating hungrily. They drank a lot of strong tea. Bo hummed and rocked, leaning against each sister in turn. They had combed his hair.

SIX

Eden checked that Brad was all right before he went to bed. He'd heard of people choking on their own vomit while they slept. He remembered the noisy sleep of the men in the barracks, the snores, groans and cries of the very drunk. 'Be content with your lot?' Most certainly not. His motto was 'Forget your past'.

Brad, having snored earlier in the lavatory, lay quiet and still. Eden tidied the blankets, refilled the hot-water bottle. Bo was asleep before the fire. Efficiency without fuss was called for, no disapproval. Bonnie's peace of mind mattered most.

'I suggest we all go to bed early. Your mother won't be back tonight, because of the storm.'

It was hotter than ever, in spite of the hail and rain earlier.

He woke with a jerk. Someone was screaming in an unearthly manner. A little wearily he wondered if one of them was being knifed. They didn't go in for half measures in this family. He felt worn out.

Bonnie and Tor were on the landing.

'It's another nightmare. He has them sometimes. All right, pet, we're coming, we're here.'

Just a dream, not a soul in torment. He sighed. He tucked his shirt in and followed them to Bo's room where he lay on his back, his eyes staring. He continued the screams, short and sharp. He was so hot his sheets and pillow were soaking, his hair was plastered flat.

'You're sure it's not a fit?' Eden asked.

'Of course not. He has nightmares. He's highly strung, aren't you, my pet?' Bonnie sat on his pillow. Together they soothed and patted him until the screams stopped.

Eden felt he was intruding, he'd felt the same that first time on the lawn. They were complete, they needed no one; grouped on the pillow, an almost holy three, intent on themselves. He looked round Bo's little room, almost a cubby hole, with a set of shelves where the window should be . . . He'd made a shrine for his prayers, there was a statue of St Patrick and some shamrock. A crucifix dangled from his rosary, his child's missal was on a shelf apart. He lay quiet now between his sisters, tuning his head to their hands that stroked. They hummed.

'All right then, Bo?' Eden felt uncomfortable.

Bo gazed at him. 'We're a lovable little family, aren't we, Eden? Do you find us curious? Do you think I'm spoiled?'

'Oh, I don't know about that.'

Bo took Tor's hand, kissing it smackingly. What a pity Bonnie was tone-deaf, poor creature; she'd never make an opera singer. Ah me.

'Would you like a hot drink?'

Eden had heard that sufferers from nightmares should be treated gently. Cocoa?

It was one thirty. The storm wasn't over yet, rolls of thunder sounded far off. Bonnie followed him downstairs. He longed to be alone with her, to tell of his admiration. To tell her to be more modest, not to sprawl at the table like that, to do up her nightdress. Some people might get the wrong idea, might take advantage. How innocent was she?

All three of them blushed easily, they had that type of skin. Tor was very likely undernourished, all three were in need of love. He wanted to button and bath them, clothe them respectably, keep them smiling and fed. He made a further resolve not to let his desire interfere with his protective feelings. They all needed him, not just Bonnie. Beautiful as she was, lust had no place.

He poured milk into a cup while she mixed cocoa and sugar.

'It's all because of Captain,' she said. 'Mamma isn't to blame.'

'I'm not blaming anyone. I don't like to see you upset.'

'I'm not upset. I'm just concerned.'

She stretched out her long legs. She had a tiny scar high on her thigh. Tor called from the landing in a loud whisper, because Captain must not wake before he'd got sober.

'What are you doing, Bonnie? Hurry.'

'She's helping make cocoa,' Eden answered. Brad wouldn't waken for hours, no need to whisper. He wanted to know about Bo's nightmares. Bonnie said they all had them sometimes, but only Bo screamed. Telling a dream when you woke was the best way to recover. Bo could never remember his. Tor's dreams were of being chased.

'And yours, Bonnie?'

Sometimes they were lovely. Gardens full of tea-roses and love-in-the-mist, small animals, butterflies that made music with their wings, bright sunlight and people dancing. Then it stopped, it went dark. It hurt. He couldn't bear to think of her in pain, she was born for sunshine and flowers. She said the dreams were worse since they'd got here, they weren't used to life in Ireland. They didn't know what lay ahead.

'I wasn't happy when I was young,' he said.

He told her about lighting Aunt's fires, about shopping for her, about trying to please, like a servant. How he'd left and never gone back. She stared at the cocoa and sugar mixture. She said that their mamma should never have married again. She had warned her; it was too late.

'I don't remember Brad drinking in the army days. Life was different. Perhaps he misses his old responsibilities.'

'Responsibilities? We are his responsibility. He's made fools of us, especially Mamma. He pretended he was rich.'

'This could be a fine property; it's small, it's been neglected, it could be restored. Do you miss your real father?'

'He died ages ago, I told you. I knew Captain would let us down. He's made Mamma miserable.'

'What are your own plans, Bonnie?'

'No more studying, thanks very much. I'll never get used to it here. Bo is happy, we are not. He loves Ireland. Mamma has changed.'

'In what way?'

'She's secretive. She cries, too. I won't marry for ages.'

'You may change. Just you wait.'

The way she blushed was sweet, Eden longed to reach for her. He asked what she liked doing.

'I wish I was a dancer, or a singer like Mamma was. But that's impossible.'

'I could teach you to dance. You mean ballroom? Stand up, Bonnie. See? We're perfectly matched.'

Now his arms were round her, sanctioned by ballroom etiquette, nothing furtive, nothing to suggest lust. He felt her thin hand, felt her backbone through her nightdress, felt her breath on his cheek. She was stiff from nervousness and ignorance but her eyes had closed. Her feet started following his. With lips just parted she looked like an angel on the brink of realizing a dream. He knew beyond doubt then that she was made for him, that he must treat her with tender care, he must adore her, must never cause sadness or pain. He increased the pressure of his arm and hand very slightly.

'I don't want to tire you, Bonnie dear. Let's go on talking for a while.'

Her breath was quick, her cheeks a sweet pink. Would he really teach her? She would love that, she said. Her mother had been on the stage, performing might be in the blood. She longed to learn to dance.

'Tell me about yourself.' He longed to know every detail, nothing was unimportant.

She said that when Bo was a baby, she and her sisters looked after him; they had taken it in turns to wheel his pram. They'd had a real garden in Yorkshire, full of flowers. They used to fill the pram with blossoms. She loved roses best, like her Mamma. Tor preferred spring flowers. He pictured them hanging their curls over the baby, the scent of primroses and violets sweet in the air. He pictured them kissing him, singing to him, playing with his toes, rocking him. He longed to kiss her himself. He would teach her to waltz, he would show her the joy of the dance. She'd had troubles early, with her first brother dying, her father dying. He'd like her to rely on him now.

'It will be wonderful, Bonnie. You're a natural mover. I think very likely we're made for each other.'

'What about Tor? Will you teach her too?'

'I will if you wish. Of course. If you like.'

'Bonnie? Bonn-ee.'

'I'll bring the cocoa. Bring the sugar in case he needs more, Bonnie . . . my dear.'

He wanted to call her his love, his angel girl, his beloved; he mustn't be impetuous.

He paused by the attic stairs to listen to Brad. He thought he heard a snore, then quiet. The sounds of sleeping people were the same, however humble or exalted their class. What mattered was their speech. He had taken particular care to speak slowly to Bonnie. He listened when the sisters spoke. Bo's fluctuating brogue was comic, his 'bedads' and 'ah me's' endearing. He himself must be word-perfect for their world. He ran over his exercise: 'Brown frowned on his way down town. He must save to pay Jane's way.' He remembered the custard cream biscuits bought earlier. Bo might like one.

His sisters watched Bo as he licked the cream fillings with his thin tongue. They piled more sugar into his cup. No wonder they had rather dingy teeth. Bonnie was still childish in many ways, Eden would see that she was happier. He had a lot to offer.

No one felt like sleeping yet, having been woken so forcibly by Bo.

'Eden, what games do you know? What word games?'

He'd never been competitive, hated all ball games. Team spirit meant nothing to him, his interest was in furthering himself. He disliked the idea of word games, they might show up his ignorance. He didn't want to risk revealing the truth about his education. Couldn't they just talk for a while?

'Let's play "Favourites". It's too late to use our brains,' Tor said quickly. Favourite animals, flowers, tunes, books, the list was endless, requiring no skill. You lost a life if you couldn't answer quickly. You must give reasons for your choice. Animals first.

'I choose my duck.'

'A duck is a bird, not a beast.'

Bo said it was the animal kingdom. Ducks found their own food. You could eat them when they got old.

'You've lost a life for being slow. I'll choose the elephant. They make good mothers and are kind.'

'I choose . . . a horse. Horses are loyal. Eden, you next.'

'Homo sapiens,' he said nervously.

'Who in particular?'

'Bonnie.'

'*Bonnie*? Sister Bonnie? Bonnie, me darlin', Eden is sweet

on you. Imagine that. Eden loves Bonnie, begorra, Eden loves Bonnie, bedad.'

Bo clutched himself, wrapping his arms tightly, rocking with mirth. His sister Bonnie, ah me.

'Stop being so rude and silly, Bo.'

Tears of shame stood in Bonnie's eyes. She leaned forward to strike him. Tor pulled her back. Bo was just joking, take no notice. Bo's mood changed, he turned to Tor, pushing his face into her hand, inviting her to stroke his hair. Darling Tor, she was his best friend. She fondled him, the highly-strung little brother.

The front door banged. The mother was back.

'Mamma? You're here. Oh Mamma. At last.'

'Sweet children. All crouched upstairs? What has been happening?'

'Captain came back. He's upstairs. He's asleep.'

She blinked slowly, she didn't seem afraid or upset. She looked faintly amused. The children were on Bo's bed, he was curled in Tor's arms. Bonnie was aloof and red.

The woman was not as Eden had imagined, not shrinking or put-upon; in the poor light she was like an older Bonnie, with coarser skin and hair. She kept her eyes wide open and taut. Her cheeks were smooth as dolls' cheeks, her mouth was lined, her hands and neck showed her age.

'Eden came, Mamma.'

She turned to him. What must he think? Had her children been looking after him? The household was somewhat *distrait* just at present; he'd come at an awkward time.

'Mamma, where were you? Are you all right?'

'Why ever not? Don't stare at me, I'm not a ghost. Please, please.' She put her hands to her face.

'We're not staring, we're just looking. We were worried,' Tor said.

'Poor sweets. All is well. Why such agitation? You got my message, I trust. I *should* have let you know sooner . . . But . . .'

'But, Mammy, you left us a long time, didn't you? We were alone. Luckily for us Eden came.'

Bo eyed his mother shrewdly. He pushed towards Tor's hand. He sighed as she wiped the cocoa stains from his mouth.

SEVEN

She was as cool as if she'd been on a holiday.

'Tell me all, my sweets. What has been happening?'

She leaned forward, her knees crossed, a high-heeled shoe dangling from one toe, another shoe under the bed. The girls were still on Bo's pillow, watching her. Were they wondering how soon she'd leave again? The plaster eyes of St Patrick watched the group from the shelf. There was no sound from Brad, upstairs.

'Bo, sweetie, did you see my purse anywhere?'

'No, Mammy.'

Eden remembered seeing him kick the purse under the bed in the attic. Did the boy steal cash to keep his father from drinking?

'Bonnie, cheer up, can't you? Why so subdued?'

'We missed you. Bo had another dream.'

'He did? Tell me, darling, what was it?'

'I don't remember. I never remember.'

Bo kept his face turned towards Tor. The mother stretched out her hand to Eden. Her skin felt dry as holly leaves.

'I *have* been remiss, haven't I? Can you forgive me?'

'That's quite all right, Mrs . . .'

'Mrs? Why so formal? Call me Babs. We are Brad and Babs, short for Barbara. My most intimate friends used to call me Bab.'

She had a secret look, as if she was thinking of the days when she'd entertained the troops. Did she still pine for the men in khaki; did she miss their stares, their admiration and whistles, the desire in their eyes? She had traded adulation for the land of shamrock, and a drunk. Her looks were fading, her children thin and sad-eyed. Her house was an overgrown shanty. Yet there was magic here, there was Bonnie. Babs saw him stare, she twitched her lips to suggest a kiss, very likely a habit from her past.

He decided that her nature was base, that her heart was as false as her pink cheeks. She was too old to be called Babs. 'Bab'? What kind of name was that? Brad had made an unwise choice. What did her daughters really think of her? They were loyal, especially Bonnie. Bo didn't pretend.

He wriggled under his sheet, screwing his face like a monkey.

'Little Babsy-wabsy. Get me a drink. I need sweet things after my dream.'

'I'll go. You stay here . . . Babs.'

No one had asked what she'd been doing or where she'd been. The Fagins lived two miles away. Now was his chance to prove his worth. He would learn Babs' needs as well as the kids'. He was getting rather sick of heating milk, of running back and forth, of shopping; he was sick of tending drunks, but he would do anything necessary, he wouldn't return to England without a fight, or unless he was fired. For Bonnie he would demean himself. One day she'd be his dancing partner. One day she'd live in the home he'd provided, with a beautiful garden of flowers.

He clanged the pan onto the stove again, he hurled more turf on the fire. That Babs woman ought to be up with her husband, checking that he was alright. He did grant that she had difficulties, but she should manage better, she'd had experience. She only seemed to think of herself.

Was she the type to drink cocoa? She was the gin-and-french class. He could see her sipping from cut glasses, nibbling cherries or olives on sticks, smiling that smile, teetering on those heels. He glanced round the kitchen; he'd wait on her like a slave, ingratiate himself. The fire, the smell of hot milk, the cloth on the table (torn but clean) were his doing. He heard those heels descending, she was coming, smiling that mouth again.

'You're supposed to be the guest, Eden. Let *me*.'

'I want to help. If I can. Anything . . . Babs.'

She looked pleased, he had called her Babs. She sat at the table, she peered at her dainty watch. What a criminal hour to be warming milk. She did appreciate his support.

'It's a pleasure. Would you like something to eat?'

There were no biscuits left and very little bread. Waiter, nursemaid, lackey, cook and bottle-washer, no matter, he would comply. If he had a lemon he'd make her Russian tea. He remembered Aunt's tray, the sight of her grey mouth, her warnings. He had proved her wrong, nothing was impossible with the right determination. How well Babs spoke, just like her daughters. Self-improvement took time and effort, he was on his way up. Goodbye loneliness. He didn't care about a stately lifestyle. He had never hunted, fished or shot at animals, never even owned a bicycle, much less an estate car. What he craved was this family's acceptance. He poured weak tea for Babs, who seemed to be giving him the come-on. It was her daughter he wanted, not her. She should be named Mrs Falseheart, with those red-tipped holly leaf hands.

'Don't rush upstairs to the infants yet, Eden. Sit down. We must talk.'

'All right, Babs. I want to be frank myself. It's about Brad. How long has he . . . ?'

'Has he what? I beg your pardon?'

'His drinking. He's upstairs, legless. I know about it. Has it been going on for long?'

'Yes, I see. I quite understand.'

Her mouth went slack, she looked at her nails. Her neck was like Bonnie's when it drooped. She was frightened inside like the others, her sophistication was an act.

'I'm not trying to interfere, Babs. How serious is it? I should know about him. He offered me a job.'

She looked up, pushing her lips fetchingly. She couldn't discuss it now, she was exhausted. The infants had obviously taken to him. She wanted him to stay.

'I was offered a position by letter. I didn't expect this. I haven't spoken to Brad about the job.'

'We are counting on you. Brad has been . . . He's had worries. It's a change from army life.'

'But the drinking . . .'

'He never did before. He needs help with the farm.'

'Farm? I must say I got a surprise.' A thin cow and a duck was hardly a farm.

'Surprise? Imagine how *I* felt. I had no idea. The state of the place. Brad misled me. Stay.'

'I will do all I can, Babs. There is certainly room for improvement.'

'Improvement? It's plague-ridden. I felt doomed as soon as we arrived.'

'Don't say that, Babs. Don't give up before you start.'

She was strong-willed, she had determination. She could get what she wanted for herself, her attic room proved that.

'There is nothing for us here. The boredom is criminal.'

'Bo seems happy. Does Brad know how you feel?'

'He knows what I'm used to, knows what I need. Any woman would be peeved.'

'I can see you're used to nice things. Your room upstairs . . . very tasteful.'

He could see that Brad hadn't turned out the magical solution to her widowhood. She had ended up in a run-down ruin in a rural area, without much means of support. They were as out of place here as an orchid in a cowpat. He asked her bluntly how often Brad got drunk.

'We never know. Not knowing is so peeving, you can't plan or rely on anything. Don't desert us.'

'I was offered a salaried position.'

'I am sure you will be paid. Brad isn't . . . we aren't destitute, you know.'

She was proud, like her children. What she said very likely wasn't true. Eden might find himself working for nothing. To help Bonnie get away he must earn money. He watched Babs, raise her cup, putting it down before drinking, making her expression appealing again.

'Babs, don't you realize how worried they were? It's lucky I come . . . I came when I did.'

'It's all very well for outsiders to find fault. You don't realize. I have tried my best. Sweet Christ, I have tried.'

'I expect Brad feels upset, he must know he's let you down, neglected all of you.'

'*I* am upset. *I'm* let down, *I'm* neglected.'

'I suppose people in different countries have different ways.'

He knew that sounded priggish, he must defend Brad if he could; he was supposed to be his boss, his provider. Why didn't he get up and come downstairs now, behave in a proper way, assume his proper place? Both he and Babs were at fault, both weak and headstrong.

Babs went on sitting there, shallow, a flirt, trembling and ogling him with those blue eyes, expecting sympathy and support. She must have dealt with heavy drinkers before now.

'You're right of course, Eden; this country *is* different. They're mad, they love their own voices, they love drinking and fighting. It's the disillusionment of my life.'

'I've hardly spoken to anyone since I got here, hardly seen anyone except this family.'

It was mission week, she said. Everything stopped. The people were in the chapel from morning till night.

'You mean Catholics? Priests?'

The Catholic church had a numbing effect, she said; the people became mesmerized by clergy and nuns. The town was taken over.

'Even Brad? Bo said nothing about any mission.'

'Booze means more to Brad than anything. Bo is a fanatical child, he'll outgrow prayers, I suppose. I sincerely hope so.'

'Is Fagin's Brad's usual haunt?'

'Fagin's? Why do you ask? What did Brad say?'

'He didn't say nothing . . . anything. Er . . . Bo was screaming something shocking while you were out. Loud screaming.'

'He's had a lot of nightmares recently. It's this benighted place.' She rubbed her thumb nail. Poor little Boris was Brad's wonder boy, his golden child, light of his life. Of course, the girls' real father was dead.

'Bonnie said. It must have been a hard time for you.'

His aunt had managed alone. Hardship was as hard as you let it be. Not that he thought anything good about Aunt.

'You probably never met a family like this one, did you? Tell me, Eden, what do you think of us?'

He felt like saying that he thought them a self-dramatizing lot of lunatics, except for Bonnie of course. He said it was too soon to make judgements. Ask again in six months' time.

'Then you'll stay. I knew you would.'

She gave him her bewitching look again, then pushed out her mouth like a kiss. In old age she'd have a tick if she wasn't careful, her type of looks didn't last. Self-interest made you insensitive. She was probably stupid too. How dare she put her children at risk.

'I'll do whatever I can.'

'Oh, you are wonderful. I worry about the girls. The anxiety . . . Bonnie . . .'

From outside the kitchen came a crash. Screams sounded from the landing. Eden leapt to his feet. They were at it again. Fresh melodrama. This lot should be on the stage. Couldn't they endure peace for five minutes?

Tor was shouting, 'Don't touch her, leave her. Let my sister alone.' Babs gave a little moan. She spilled her tea, catching her heel in the blue table-cloth, smashing her cup to the ground. Sweet Christ, she was doomed.

Feet on the stairway, bodies falling, a chair falling, a crash, another scream. Eden was there. If anyone laid a finger on Bonnie . . . Brad was in his shirtsleeves, grappling with her, falling, losing her, grabbing her.

'Little bitch, I'll teach you to meddle with my things. Stay out of my room.'

Eden felt that his eyes and ears were bursting. He wanted to kill Brad with his bare hands.

'Let her go, or you won't live to remember. Let go of her, I said.'

He shoved Brad against the banisters. He put his arms round Bonnie. Darling, dear one, he was there.

He felt teeth biting his knuckles. Bo was screaming at him now. Don't dare threaten his father, don't touch him. Dadda couldn't help himself. There, Dadda, there.

'It's me. It's Bo. I'm here.'

Brad leaned back against the stair rail. He slipped down, he sat on the bottom step. His eyes were without guile or malice again before he closed them. Whatever had angered him was forgotten. Babs, still in the kitchen, stood twisting her hands. It was criminal, it was all too much to bear.

'I'll get him upstairs again, don't worry.'

Eden dragged him by the armpits.
'He can't help himself, he won't remember,' Bo said.
Babs stayed where she was. Tor had her arms round Bonnie who was in tears.

Brad's hand caught in the banisters, Eden dragged him free. Let his wrist break, he deserved it. Eden wished he had choked on his vomit. Still, it was another chance to prove his ability. He would provide food and drink, create heat, calm nightmares, shop and clean, reassure the anxious, escort drunkards to their beds.

A whisky bottle under Brad's pillow was a clue to the outburst. Apparently the two girls had gone up, Brad had woken to find Bonnie taking the whisky. Was she in danger? He must get her away as soon as possible, settle her, make her happy, teach her dancing. His angel dance-partner-to-be.

He tucked Brad firmly into bed again. He took the whisky and went down. Babs was in Bo's room with her daughters, let her attend to them. The kitchen was quiet. It was after three in the morning, he wasn't doing any more for anyone. He finished the whisky. The fire was out. Let it stay out, he wasn't getting on his knees again.

He straightened the cloth, picked up the broken china. His hand still felt sore from Bo's teeth. He sucked his knuckle. On the floor was a splash of blood. He bent down; it wasn't blood, but one of Babs' thumbnails, false and shining. He threw it onto the ashes in the fireplace where it glowed like a scarlet flower.

EIGHT

'Eden, wake up. It's late.'

'Whassat? Sorry, Aunt. I must have slep' it out. I'll get your tea.'

'Who is "Aunt"? What are you talking about? This is Tor.'

'Oh . . . Sorry, Tor. Of course. I forgot where I was for a minute.'

The present came back to him. This was Ireland. He had slept late after drinking Brad's whisky, he wasn't with Aunt in Streatham, he would never go back there again. He was living with gentry, on his way to belonging with them. He was at the Grange. He blinked at Tor, feeling dazed. For all he knew, Aunt might be dead now, and her warnings with her. Had his grammar let him down again?

'Is it raining? What's that din, Tor?'

She looked spectral in the light of his bedroom. The rain had got worse, they were being flooded out. The roof was leaking, rain was seeping under the window sills and over the doorsteps; they were in danger of being washed away. Listen to it, that noise was rain. The lights didn't work, the turf in the shed was wet through.

'I never knew Irish weather could be like this.'

Torrents streamed down the window pane, rattling on the skylight outside, dripping onto the landing. No wonder the place smelled like graves. He shivered, still half awake. He mustn't be morbid, there was work to do, there was Bonnie to look after.

'Has anyone been up to Brad again?'

'Mamma stayed with us in Bo's room. It's better if he's left alone.'

Before Eden went down he paused to listen for Brad's breathing. He felt responsible. Babs should have been to him. He would check again, make sure.

Brad was lying in the same position as when he'd left him, his nose tilting towards his pillow, his hands slack on the sheet. His breathing was laboured now, sounding harsh and painful. Eden leaned over him. His lips were blue. Rain was dripping onto the bedclothes through the attic skylight. Brad didn't move as Eden pulled the bed out of the way.

'Wake up, Brad. Sober up, can't you? You're soaked. The family need you. You can't lie here forever.'

He rubbed his hands, he shook him. Brad was inert.

In the kitchen Babs was holding bread to the fire; she moved awkwardly, she held her fork awkwardly as if unused to kitchen chores. There was no more turf in the baskets. Bo was scrabbling for any bits he could find, throwing them into the grate to make a brief flare. His piece of toast lay in the hearth, blackened. He whined to Tor for jam.

'Give me some in the spoon, you creature. I want some. Now.'

'I don't think Brad is well. Have you seen him, Babs?'

'Seen him? I've been trying to cope with all this on my own. What with Bo's whines and Bonnie's sulks, I've had enough. He's doubtless drunk still.'

Babs' face was white, she wore no lipstick, her thumbnail gleamed as pale as the bread she was holding.

'I lit the fire for you, Mammy. I want some jam now please.'

'I'm worried about his breathing, Babs. The roof has leaked onto him. The bed is soaked. I felt I should look at him, I'm glad I did. I hope you don't object.'

'Object? Why should I? Do what you like. I'm on my knees.' Babs waved the fork, dropping the last piece of bread.

Bonnie turned from the window.

'Sulking? I'm not sulking. I hate you. I hate everything. I'm sick of you all.'

'I'm afraid that Brad may have the flu, Babs.'

'Flu? Good. He deserves it after last night. You've seen how he drinks. His chest is weak.'

'Poor Dadda, he couldn't help it. He isn't well, you know that, Mammy.'

'Mamma, shouldn't you explain to Eden about Captain having been in the hospital?'

'Shut your mouth, Tor. Don't talk about it.'

Bo clawed at Tor with his nails, trying to bite her.

'What happened, Tor. If Brad has been ill I should ought to know about it.'

'Don't ask questions. Mind your business. Give me some jam, you cur.'

'There's no more jam, pet, we finished it yesterday. We should tell Eden, he ought to know.'

'Tell me what, Tor? Explain it, please.'

He tried not to speak fast in the heat of the moment. In a quiet voice Tor explained that Brad had been in the local hospital this summer because of his alcoholism.

'I did ought to get the doctor then. Now.'

'You're not to. I won't let you. Cur.' Bo was screeching.

Babs put her head in her hands. Did the child have to make that noise?

'Let me go for the doctor, Babs. Bo can come with me, may he?'

'Do what you like. Get your raincoat, Bo.' He could go anywhere he liked for peace.

Bonnie looked at her mother. His raincoat? What raincoat? None of them had any clothes worth the name. Babs was supposed to have bought them clothes when they got to Ireland. They had little more than what they stood up in. *Clothes?* Really, Mamma, think again.

'Enough, Bonnie. My head.'

Eden went for his demob. raincoat and stout ex-officer's shoes. He'd be quicker going alone, in any case. This place was bedlam. Babs was a disaster, with her selfishness and false red nails. The doctor would be out very likely, lurking in some pub or church. Mission week? Disaster week was more like it. Week of doom, week of drinking, week of floods.

He fingered the cheque book in his pocket. The prospect of increasing his bank balance looked increasingly remote. How shocked his aunt would be over this lot. But he didn't regret coming to Ireland, far from it. Land of dreams, land of romance, Bonnie's land. He would practise his elocution exercise as he walked in the rain again. 'Brown frowned.'

A car was moving through the storm, jerkingly, starting and stalling. An old Morris Minor came into view, drawing up under his window. Black-trousered legs appeared and a vast umbrella. He heard the door bell ring.

'Eden? Could you come down, please?'

What did Babs want? It couldn't be the doctor.

The parish priest was in the hall. He had pushed past Babs, was shaking his umbrella. He had large ears and teeth, he wore galoshes over his shoes.

'Is Bradwell about? Tell him I'm come if you please, Marm.'

'I'm afraid not. You can't see him. He can't see you.'
Her voice wavered. Dislike and fear showed in her eyes.
'Is that right for a fact, Marm? May I ask the reason why?'
'Can I help, Babs?'
'This is Eden, Father. He's Bradwell's new manager. Bradwell is unwell. Eden comes from London.'
'London? So? And how are you now, sir? If Bradwell is poorly he'll want to see me. I'll just take a run upstairs.'
'Father, I have just said, he isn't well. He's asleep.'
'His usual complaint, I take it. I was afraid of that when he wasn't at Mass. He's not been near the chapel since the mission started. He'll be wanting to see me now, Marm.'
Babs looked to Eden for support. This man must not be allowed upstairs. Bottles, soaking furniture, frippery and frills in her room.
'Er . . . perhaps you could call later, Father, when he's better? He's not up to visitors yet.'
'Out of my way, sir. Are you plotting to keep a man of the cloth from his flock? Stand clear, let me pass.'
'No, Father. As Brad's wife I refuse to allow it. There is no need.'
'Marm, if your husband has had a slip I need to know about it. There is indeed the need.'
'Slip? Dadda is quite well thank you, Father.'
Bo was in the hall, his blackened toast crust in his hand. He must speak to the Father urgently.
'Wait now, boy. After I've been upstairs.'
'I want to come. Dadda will need me.'
Babs grabbed his arm. 'Stand still. Hold your tongue, don't interfere.'
Eden wanted to tell Babs that Bo felt excluded. He wanted to be with his father, he felt apprehensive. Babs was concerned with being in charge. She ran from her intolerable life when she felt like it, yet she needed to rule, needed power. The Father was a threat to her control; the church's

word was law, no one could stop him going up. The attic door closed, they could hear nothing. Was the priest murmuring prayers for the sick, administering the final rites? Touching Brad with oil and water, blessing, absolving in Latin, making the sign of the Cross? Suffering and excitement seemed necessary to this family, if Brad died they'd be lost. Eden smothered another yawn of weariness, he mustn't flag. Diligence, attentiveness, watch your speech. Each new crisis is another chance to prove your worth.

The attic door opened again, they heard the squelch of the Father's galoshes on the stairs; his ears, teeth and bald head came into view.

'No question about it, Marm. I'm experienced in the way of sickness. It's the hospital for Bradwell, right away.'

'I beg your pardon. Allow me to decide what is . . . It's my husband, remember.'

'And my parishioner, Marm. I am his parish priest. Remember that if you will.'

'I won't allow you . . .'

'Allow me to judge what is best. Was it not me that christened him? 'Twas a mercy I came when I did.' The Father closed his teeth with a snap, scowling at Babs.

'Do you expect me to go on my knees to you? You waltz in without invitation, you start laying down the law.'

'Stop, stop, Mammy. Don't argue with the Father. I must talk to him.'

'Wait now, boy, shortly. You're to start with the Brothers next term. I have it arranged for you. Your Dadda must come with me now.'

Eden spoke slowly and clearly. Might it not be best if Brad went now with the Father in his car? He had seen Brad himself, he did seem very ill. As he spoke he moved out of range of Bo in case he had another tantrum, he wasn't risking those teeth again. There'd been enough combat and violence for the moment. A little ordinary courtesy wouldn't come amiss. He might be expected to make tea for the priest. But Bo was quiet, he'd got his wish, he was to start at the school of his choice, thanks to the priest.

'Pleurisy, Marm; you had thought of that? Bronchitis? Quinsy?'

'Yes, yes. I quite understand. His chest is weak. We know.'

'I'll take him with me now.'

Babs was silent. Perhaps that would be best, easier all round.

'I'm glad, Marm, that you can see reason.'

The priest looked at her with distaste. Protestant woman that she was, without thought for anyone or anything but her own pleasure. Dilatory, neglectful, wrong-headed and, if gossip had it right, loose in her ways. She was apt to visit Fagin's farm a shade too often. That Mick one at the bar encouraged Bradwell in drink. It was high time the Fagin brothers found wives of their own. Nothing like a wife to keep a man straight. This Protestant one was in another class, from what he'd heard tell. Not that he encouraged scandal, but a priest had a duty to know. The likes of this one and her daughters were a blot on the parish. English, heathen, with time on their hands. The young lad, now, was different; a soul waiting to be snatched from danger. He was unruly, lacking manners, with a nasty temper, but the Christian Brothers would set him right. Marrying outside the church had been Bradwell's ruin, on top of going to England to fight; such action brought no good result.

Tor called her brother. 'Come on, pet, help me now.'

There was work to do if Captain was leaving with the Father. Someone must prepare hot-water bottles for his journey, he must be kept warm. He must have a thermos of tea for the trip. While Bonnie sulked behind her hair, she and Bo would help.

Babs was on her dignity. Naturally she would travel with

her husband, she would sit in front by the priest while Brad stretched out in the back. Later she would return with his clothes in a suitcase. The rule of the hospital was that all lockers must be kept empty until the patient's discharge. Without his clothes Brad would be safely contained. Eden thought it unlikely that she'd visit him.

Tor and Bo put bottles, rugs and cushions in the back of the car. Eden and the Father lifted and dragged Brad downstairs. His face looked dreadful, his breath rasped. As Tor wound a scarf round him he moaned.

'Hush, Captain, you're going to hospital.'

'Disaster. Where is . . . she?'

Bo did up his shoes. Not to worry, he'd look after things at home until Dadda was back.

'Out of the way, children.'

Babs wore a lavender woollen coat with a nipped waist. The turned-up collar framed her face, she looked queenly.

'Oh, my gloves. Bonnie, be a lamb.'

Bonnie handed them through the window. Babs smiled. Such a thoughtful daughter.

'Weather for ducks.' The Father sighed, adding, 'God bless all here.'

Babs smoothed her lavender kid gloves over her fingers. Father's ears shone like signals in the gloom of the car. He settled his galoshes comfortably. He turned the starter. Brad didn't move. No one waved or said goodbye. They were gone.

Eden slumped against the hall door. Just him and the kids again, time for a breathing space, he hoped. Time to do something about the leaks.

'Come on, then. I'll show you how to keep the rain out.'

First they must put pots and pans under the roof leaks on the landing. Tor and Bo routed under the stairs. They found rags under a basket of empty bottles and newspaper. Eden showed them how to wrap rags round wads of paper, to push into the cracks round the windows. There was no fire, no electricity, but the tension was easier. Soon the sound of raindrops falling into the various containers upstairs made an odd, syncopated beat.

'What shall I do, Eden?'

'Stay by me. Hold this. We'll stay upstairs until your mother gets back. Bo's room is the best.'

Bo lay round his duck on his bed, protecting it. Tor lay next to him. They were curled like spoons.

'Bonnie? Don't look so sad.'

'You mustn't judge Mamma, Eden. I know her best. She changed when we came here.'

'She told me she found it difficult. It's you I want to help.'

Bonnie of the beautiful eyes must trust him.

By the time Babs got back, Bo was over-tired, over-excited and obnoxious. His sisters were trying to calm him when she appeared.

'Must you sing like that, Bonnie? The noise. What is that bird doing here?'

'Mammy, is Dadda all right?'

'Don't bother me. I'm going up.'

'Someone was in the lodge, Mammy. Someone has been there.'

'You nasty little boy, hold your tongue. Let me get some sleep.'

Eden wondered how someone like that could produce someone like Bonnie. Could anyone soften her? She was inhuman.

It was the last time they saw her alive.

NINE

As long as I can remember I have felt older than Bonnie, older even than Mamma. I have heard of people having old souls; you are born like that. I may have lived other lives before this one. I feel older and wiser inside. I don't remember feeling young, not like Bo or Ula. I was always aware of adult strain.

Ula missed that summer at the Grange. Mamma had planned to settle us in Ireland, then return to Ula to see what could be done to bring her over. But Mamma died instead.

Until we left England, Bonnie and I were close; we didn't need anyone else. We had experienced death early, our real father first, then our first brother as an infant, then our headmistress at boarding school. Ula had killed her best friend by accident when she was seven. (The friend had fallen under Ula's penknife.) You might think that Ula would be scarred for life, but she grew up a cheerful soul. Our parents going away was worse than anything; you mind them leaving when you're very young, it's worse than death, in a way. I used to know Bonnie's thoughts before Ireland. Then she changed.

Bo loved the Grange. He was a braggart; it would all come to him one day, he was Captain's one blood child, he'd be the owner. He was always a show-off and a pampered brat. Bonnie and I hated the Grange.

She had warned Mamma about marrying Captain. We didn't take to him, my sisters and I disliked most men. Men were better ignored, they rarely understood children. Their wars, their news on the wireless, their money problems, weren't our affair. If they didn't try to understand us, why need we understand them? Mamma had flattered Bonnie into approving of her wedding by making her a bridesmaid. Ula and I had watched from the front pew as Mamma and Captain made their promises and Bonnie stood behind. I wanted Bonnie to trip, to disgrace the ceremony, but it went off without a mistake. The three of them looked gilded with joy. Ula and I wore high-waisted frocks and felt out of place. Bonnie's swishing chiffon and little bolero with flowers was a paler blue than Mamma's. They wore ringlets and high-heeled shoes, unreal as fashion plates. Mamma read a lot of magazines but hated books. Clothes and make up were her passion, as well as popular war-time songs. Her favourite song was 'You'd be So Nice to Come Home to.' I pitied her when Captain so often did not come home.

Bonnie had turned to us during the service, smiling back in triumph. Mamma confided in her, she knew her secrets. Ula and I were too young to discuss lipstick, bosoms and having babies. Mamma had chosen her.

I remember Captain at the reception, holding his glass tightly in his hand. His eyes were fixed on Mamma adoringly, the drink in his hand mattered, too. Mamma was affected as usual; wriggling her shoulders, blinking behind her eye veil with the flowers sewn on it. She puffed smoke through a long cigarette holder, she smiled too hard, her eyes were hard behind that flowery veil.

'Where is that handsome husband of mine? Bonnie, did you steal him away? She's my eldest you know, isn't she pretty?'

The guests smiled and toasted the gilded couple and the bridesmaid, yellow bubbles sparkled in the glasses. Bonnie clung to Captain as if she were the bride, loving the limelight. At that moment she believed that he was our passport to family happiness. She was the prettiest, Mamma's favourite, Captain would love her best. A ringlet curled round a flower on her bolero, she was pink-cheeked, with the world in her hand.

For Captain, Mamma had given up entertaining the forces, for him she'd become the mother of Bo. He was born in Yorkshire; our joy, our delight, from birth Bo realised his power. We competed to hold him, to wash and feed him, our lives revolved round his baby smiles. Captain was posted abroad, we lived in a bungalow. Mamma looked after us in a half-hearted way. She tried to make soup from rabbit bones, complaining that cooking roughened her hands. She taught us to file our nails horizontally, drawing the file downwards to strengthen the growth. We had to write polite letters to Captain in Tunisia, to use pumice stone on the soles of our feet. Her own bedroom was always beautiful, but the home in Yorkshire never felt really clean. We used to love the garden; an old man came to tend the flowers. Playing in that garden became my happiest memory. We used to make immensely long daisy chains for Bo. Mamma used to order expensive clothes from London for us. If you had money clothes rationing didn't hinder you. She should have stocked up for Ireland. Instead, we left everything. We had left Yorkshire with romantic hopes and expectations.

In some ways Bonnie was like Mamma. I think she expected to run round Ireland in a peasant blouse and green flannel, a colleen in a story, with black hair streaming in the wind.

We had expected luxury in Ireland. What we found gave us a shock. Captain had lied about his stately home; it wasn't a mansion, there were no servants, no lovely grounds. The food was poor, there were no landed gentry near, no neighbours of any kind except the Fagin brothers two miles away. I don't know what Captain had done before the war, perhaps he just lurked in Fagin's Bar.

Bonnie minded a lot about it, she'd so looked forward to new Irish clothes. She moped in her mirror, combing her hair; she cut her toenails and scrutinized her bust. I have always loved reading, but there were no books here. I wrote in my diary. Peace-time brought no improvement to our lives.

As well as having the old soul, I was the smallest and thinnest. I missed Ula, who had been ill for over a year; I worried about her. Being different from other families seemed a serious worry. Captain had turned out a serious disappointment. It's difficult to feel proud of a drunk.

Bonnie didn't know what she did want. She hated studying, she refused to do it. I wanted to be a nurse. I hadn't told Mamma or Captain about it, they were too busy with their own affairs. They rowed, they wouldn't speak to each other, they shut themselves in their room. And all the time we waited. When would he get drunk again? Our hair, our clothes, the state of our teeth, didn't matter to Mamma now. We felt we were a source of shame. We used to listen to them shouting in the attic, sometimes we hid in the barn with the thin cow for company. At other times they smiled into each other's eyes like they had at their wedding; they went up, they shut the attic door and we heard nothing. In a way those silent times were worst. It comforted me to think of being a nurse.

When Captain left and didn't come back for days, it was a relief at first. What you dreaded had happened, the waiting was over. Then he came back and it started again. Worst of all was if Mamma went too. I suppose she went to make him feel guilty. He drove her to it, was he satisfied? When she came back she stayed in her attic, crying and sleeping. She didn't cook now, not even rabbit bone soup. Sometimes she let Bonnie up there for limbering exercises and talk about make up. Mamma worried about her neck, her bust and thighs. We tried not to let Bo see we were worried, he liked babyish games and being spoiled.

He defended Captain, his own blood father from whom one day he'd inherit the Grange. He said that Captain drank because of money worries, his debts were awful. Mamma was extravagant. There was something going on between her and Mick Fagin. Captain was jealous as well as troubled.

Since we got here, Bo started stealing. He didn't spend the money he took, he hid it or threw it away. I found seven-and-six once, in the barn by the duck's nest, another time there was a pile of pennies by the gate. He bit and spat if you questioned him, he could be vicious as well as a brat. When his front tooth was loose he bit Bonnie, leaving the tooth stuck in her thigh. He was terrified of being sent to school in England where he wouldn't know what was happening. However awful, not knowing was worse than knowing. You knew where you were if you knew the truth. I suppose that was why he was so religious, sucking up to the priest, saying his prayers in a loud voice in order to be sent to the Christian Brothers. It must be terrible to have to love your own father and your religion exaggeratedly in order not to be sent away. He ran round kissing Captain and rattling his rosary. His brogue was another pretence. He was always happy when Bonnie and I sang to him, though Bonnie had a hideous voice. I was glad that Ula didn't know about our problems; she'd been quite ill for a long time. She'd probably have to wear a leg iron when she came out of hospital. Bo said he looked forward to pushing her round in the dolls' pram. Poor old cripple, he'd teach her some prayers.

Mamma had always hated religion, I suppose she was afraid of it, the church had so much power. She said that guilt and remorse gave you frown-lines, the past was dead, why fret about life to come? You made your own heaven or hell in the present. People should be free to make up their own minds. She didn't approve of the Brothers' school; they ruled by fear, they instilled lies. Bo should avoid all such holy nonsense and go to a proper English school. Mamma was small-minded, she neglected us, she was selfish, but we needed her. I longed to be able to admire her, she was all we had.

Eden, having known Captain in the army, might be a good influence on him, might even stop him drinking. When I first saw him, his appearance was a surprise. Captain had a ferret-face with blue stubble on it when he needed to shave. When sober he was dapper and neat. You couldn't imagine Eden looking slipshod. It was a hot day when he arrived, but he looked cool. His moustache was the soft kind, not bristling, growing from fine, soft skin. His straight hair was fine too. He looked too frail for manual work, but he seemed determined and sensible. We needed someone to curb Captain's wild schemes when he got drunk. He ranted about breeding Guernsey cattle for export, or training greyhounds for racing. With whisky, his imagination soared. Eden looked down to earth, he might induce Mamma to forget Mick Fagin and attend to her duties.

He was by the laurel bushes when I first saw him, a man with a cheap suitcase and ordinary mac, listening and watching. He wasn't tall, he looked reliable, that was the main thing. Bonnie pretended not to see. She liked showing her legs and her figure off. Pretty Bonnie always had style.

Mamma didn't like her using make up, she used a lead pencil round her eyes, blinking them the way Mamma did. Bonnie got the best presents; seed pearls, watches, a little ring when she was bridesmaid, like Mamma's ring, with opals and rubies, shaped like a flower. Mamma loved jewelry, her make up was expensive, like her clothes, mostly French. She wanted Bonnie as a confidante, yet she wanted to keep her a child. Coming to Ireland changed Mamma, she seemed rather pathetic, a figure of tragedy, often she was sad.

I have kept a diary since I could first write. Memories get confused, you can trust the written word. People fail or betray you, the diary is a constant friend. I suppose keeping one helped my old soul to develop. The one I had at that boarding school is so crammed the pages look black. The writing reflects joy or unhappiness, I have never missed a day. We used to long for letters from Mamma when she was away. Entertaining troops took all her attention, until Captain entered her life.

I wanted to join her and Bonnie in the attic room, all trailing with Mamma's lovely things, but they didn't need anyone else. When Captain came home drunk, Bonnie was excluded. She joined Bo and me and we listened to them downstairs. Mamma was contemptuous of his greyhound and Guernsey cow schemes, they were the ravings of a madman. He accused her of lack of confidence, she and her children kept him poor. She was extravagant, a millstone, useless. She didn't plead or wail, she retaliated. Look what I gave up. For what? You've dragged me down. Then the front door would slam again and he'd go back to the town. Sometimes Mamma would leave then. We didn't ask her to stay, we didn't ask her where she went.

Bo became addicted to sugar in Ireland. I've seen him steal sweets from the Co-op. Once he stole a bottle of gin, I found it under some hay in the barn. Pretty Bonnie got more selfish, but she was fond of Bo, she was loyal.

Marrying a person for protection is a poor reason. Mamma should have waited until she'd seen his home. I expect he would have been a drunkard in any case, but Mamma tried to make him feel small. The Grange was rotting; it must have been nice once. Bo loved it with all his Irish soul.

Mamma must have realized her mistake when she saw those broken white gates, the state of the lodge and the drive. No sign of affluence or even comfort. Captain didn't own a bicycle, let alone a car. How could we shop for our clothes? The one bus to the city left at dawn each day. She didn't speak. We passed the lodge and the laurel bushes, we saw the Grange. Mamma went up to the attic and closed the door. Captain arrived later, having lingered in Fagin's Bar. Once when Mamma left us, the bar closed too. We wondered about that.

I remembered the way Captain had gripped his glass at the reception, the first time he came home drunk. He had that same soft look, he moved slowly, he looked at Bonnie in a special way, his accent was more pronounced, he spoke with deliberation.

'Before any-thing is said on the subject of lateness, I apol-ogize. I was delayed. It will not happen . . . again.'

'You're drunk.'

'Wait, now. Ah wait. Hold your horses. I was delayed. Business. The subject is . . . closed.'

'Is that all you have to say? I have plenty to say I assure you.'

'Now, Babsie, don't take that att-itude. I've been making a deal. Guernsey herd. It can't fail, I tell you. Give me a couple of years . . . 's'going to change. You'll see.'

'Change? How? Absurd dreams of greyhounds and cows? Your mind is addled with whisky and self-impor-tance. I suggest you go upstairs before you fall.'

'I will, Babsie me darling, if you will come with me. Come on up now for a wee lie down.'

He needed a shave, his shirt was grimy, he half fell as he tried to stand. Where was Mamma's dashing officer? He was frightening us. Worse, he was frightened himself.

'Filthy peasant. Look at you. How dare you? Haven't you humiliated me sufficiently?'

'Peasant, am I? You didn't think so once. I was good enough to take on your brats. Peasant, is it? Humil-iated? On your dig-nity? I see.'

'There is little dignity about life here, I can assure you.'

'Then why stay? You were keen enough in the first place.'

'Look at it. A pigsty. Damp and debris. A disgrace.'

The shouting went on. Captain threw a plate on the floor. Bonnie was crying.

I had been right. Mamma had made a mistake. The bank manager wouldn't cash cheques, the Co-op refused credit, we could only shop at Fagin's Bar. By the time Eden came, we needed shoes as well as clothes. We had one comb between us, we had to wash with kitchen soap. Mamma had stopped wriggling and simpering for Captain long ago, now she watched him with unloving eyes. My periods stopped. Bo stole. Bonnie wasn't my friend.

When I saw Eden watching us on the lawn, I guessed that he'd be our lifeline. He stared at Bonnie, who had her blouse open. She looked brazen, the sun glinted on her tangled hair. His friendly eyes and soft moustache even seemed familiar. He flicked back a lock of hair with his fingers. I may have seen him in a regimental photograph. Soldiers had never interested me. We had been urged to knit for them, Mamma had sung for them, they fought a war that adults loved. They pretended to hate it, war excited them. They prayed for peace, when it came they complained that the old days had gone. Peace for our family was a nightmare. Captain and Mamma quarrelled, we had nothing to do. Now here was Eden from London, watching us; an Englishman with a soft moustache and silky hair.

'Look, Bonnie, someone is here.'

Eden's grammar went wrong sometimes, I don't think Bonnie or Bo noticed. What Bonnie cared about was being noticed and admired. She was the least resourceful. I had my diaries and my nursing plans. Bo dreamed of being a Catholic landowner, restoring the Grange which would be his. Also he might be a priest. He liked writing rather bad rhymes.

He said he'd give hunt balls to which his sisters could come. Bonnie sniffed; priests didn't give balls. Bo said he'd do what he liked. He'd have a peacock lawn and a gazebo where he'd write verses and Bonnie was just envious.

She had dreamed once herself of ancestral halls with polished floors. She told me about it in Yorkshire while she practised dancing, with a cushion for a partner. In the dream, an orchestra of violins softly played, while outside a moon waited to shine on kissing couples. At school we had learned a kind of jitterbugging from some evacuees who were there. Bonnie wanted to waltz with a handsome suitor, so far she'd not had one. There was no one that Mamma would have considered suitable here, no one of standing. I suppose she wanted us to marry well.

It was when Captain tried to attack Bonnie that I knew Mamma wanted her out of the way. Bonnie might grow to be a threat. Poor Bonnie, who Mamma loved best.

'Look, Bonnie, someone is here.'

Someone to trust, someone anxious to please, someone to take over. I trusted my instinct, my old soul was a good judge.

Eden had helped us through the difficult time. Without him we might have all been drowned. He took over the mopping up, he kept the rain at bay. The Father took Captain and Mamma away, Eden showed us how to roll paper and rag together to stuff into crannies, to put pans under the leaks, to sweep the wet from the steps. Some of the rags were old knickers, the newspapers smelled of cats. We must keep dry, he said. What food did we like best? Bonnie said in a strained voice that she wasn't hungry, she was still upset from the row in the hall.

'Worried about your figure, sister darlin'? I fancy a little sandwich myself, with honey.' Bo was partial to jelly too.

It would be evening before Mamma returned, the hospital was some miles away. Bo strutted about, with his parents away he was boss again. Bow down, slaves, to your lord and master; don't forget who would inherit the Grange. Bonnie watched him with clear eyes. I wished she would talk. People shouldn't bottle up their feelings after upsets. Bo was usually impossible, he showed off, he was arrogant, he stole, bit, screamed like a pampered upstart. It was better than silence.

That night we played games again. I guessed that Eden couldn't spell, had left school when very young. He liked working with his hands, had never been a swot. Bo said he would become an Irish scholar, a local saint even, and a poet. We would draw ghosts and monsters on old envelopes. He would start first with a banshee.

'Look, Eden. You do one.'

Bonnie began to relax as she watched. She would do a goblin. Banshees were bad luck.

'No, no. It's squealing. Look, Eden.'

Eden looked at Bonnie, he felt her hand. Was she warm enough? He put a blanket round her shoulders. He lit a candle in a saucer on the floor. She was a candlelit beauty, a colleen with brilliant eyes. When it was too dark to draw, Bo said he'd make shadows for us. He'd make a banshee, look, Eden, a shrieking banshee. Ay-eee.

'You'll frighten the duck, Bo. Don't.'

He started turning cartwheels.

'Calm down, Bo. Don't get excited.'

'I bought some lemonade early. I'll get it.'

A fizzy drink in a stone bottle. Bo was charmed. A bottle of champagne bubbly. Sham pain? Anyone like some real pain? He staggered, he rolled his eyes, he was drunk. Look, everyone, drunk as a lord, getting drunker. He sang in a falsetto wail.

'I'm forever blowing bubbles, and I am a drunk old man. Me and my duck never had much luck, my daughters are sad, my wife is mad . . .'

'Stop at once, Bo. How can you?'

He couldn't stop, he was carried away, an entertainer, a poet, a mimic, look everyone, he was like his dadda. I could see his sad eyes in the light of the candle, despairing, almost crying. Wasn't he funny? Wasn't he clever; he couldn't stop. 'My daughters are mad, my wife is sad.'

And then Mamma was back again. Stop, Bo, she mustn't hear.

'Out of your minds? Must you make that noise? That bird . . .'

'Mammy, is Dadda all right?'

'Don't bother me, I'm going up.'

'Someone was in the lodge, Mammy. Someone was there.'

'Nasty little boy. Hold your tongue. That noise. I'm going up.'

Had she brought Captain's clothes back? How long would peace last this time?

Shreds of skin had curled from her lower lip. Her mauve eyelids had aged. Had the Father spoken to her about Mick Fagin? If he had, we would never know. She was dead in the morning. The attic skylight blew in and killed her; she was hit on the head, she choked with rain water, having taken pills.

Bonnie and I were not the same after that. My old soul left

childhood behind for good. We decided not to say 'Mamma' again. She would be 'she' or 'Babs', but not Mamma. It would be better if we avoided mentioning her until we felt more settled. We would probably miss her one day, but you don't miss what you never had.

TEN

'Don't let Bo in. Don't let him see.'

I had gone first to the attic to see if she wanted tea.

Only yesterday I'd come up here with Bonnie behind me, and Captain had gone berserk. Now he was banished to the hospital and our mother lay still as a stone.

Last night after she left us, the candle burned into a pool of grease, we felt shivery. Eden said that by morning life would look brighter, we were all over-tired, come along, early bed. The candle smoke smelled bitter. Eden said he'd be up early to try to get a fire going with wet turf mould. We'd been missing sleep lately. Bonnie and I were glad to be in bed.

She was still sleeping when I got up next morning, pale and beautiful. It was just before we fell asleep that we'd made our decision not to say 'Mamma' again. She wasn't the type of mother we needed. Better to look on her as a kind of neighbour, or better still an elderly aunt. We wouldn't write the name 'Mamma', we wouldn't think it.

The rain had stopped in the morning. I felt pleased that Eden was here.

'Bonnie. Bon-nee. Come quickly. Don't let Bo come. Don't let him see.'

She was lying in a mess of plaster and pieces of glass; there were tiles from the roof over the bed. Her eyes were still open, her mouth looked terrible; a shrivelled, miserable hole. The dried blood over one eyebrow looked like mud, the rose-coloured shawl round her shoulders was soaked. The eyes were the worst, they looked accusing. By her head was something wet and furry. Some animal must have come through the roof, a rat or a squirrel had been knocked senseless, but I couldn't worry about that now. Bonnie must help me take the debris off her. A brick must have cut her head. She had no protection from the weather, though the storm was over.

'Get Eden. Don't tell Bo.'

We were experiencing another death, I must stay clearheaded and practical. I had the old soul. Bonnie was shaking again. We must get a doctor or an ambulance. If she were dead, she'd need an undertaker. We'd have to pay a huge amount for flowers. She had loved roses. Did proper roses grow in Ireland or only wild ones? Where was the funeral parlour? They were all Catholic; Babs would hate that, she wouldn't like the Father praying about her. I remembered my dead baby brother lying stiff and cold as Babs was now.

Bonnie was watching with a sick-looking face.

'Stop looking like that. Don't tell Bo. Get Eden.'

But he'd seen. He came behind Eden, he saw the room, he saw the bed, he screamed. He flung himself on her, he rolled her. Wake up. Stop that. Open up your eyes.

'Now listen, Mamma, time to be up and about. Open those eyes and stop playing. Joke over, you hear me? This is Bo, it's orders.'

'She can't. Stop it, Bo. She can't hear. Leave her.'

'Take your hands off me, don't touch me. She *can* hear. She's playing a joke.'

'She can't, Bo. She's . . .'

'She can. She can.'

He put his face to the face on the bed, he rocked her back and forth.

'Listen. Hear that? She's breathing.'

From inside Babs came squelching sounds. He heaved and rolled harder. She was full of liquid inside.

'I told you. I told you. She's alive.'

Her pill bottle was by her, pills were everywhere. She looked so dead. I hoped she hadn't felt the bricks falling or heard the plaster and glass.

Bo turned on Eden. 'It's your fault. Everything is your fault. You keep telling us what to do, you keep explaining. We were all right till you came.'

'Eden is trying to help.'

'We don't want his help. And you can shut up, you fat cow.'

He lunged at me, I didn't blame him. Scratching and biting helped him.

He cried then, falling on top of Babs.

'Don't, Bo. There, there. Don't.'

'Sacred heart of . . . what is this? Has Mammy had some kind of an animal in her bed? Look at that.'

I thought only old people wore hair pieces. She'd had one all along and we'd not guessed, the same glinty shade as her real hair, like a squirrel or a rat or even a little fur crown.

We placed it over her temples, patting it lightly; we arranged a curl over the gash on her brow. She could harm us no more, we must be respectful. Her chin was wet, her eyes stared. As we settled her I knew that she'd not disliked us; we'd just bored her, we weren't exciting. Some people shouldn't have children too young. I wished we'd not discovered the hairpiece or the teeth under the bed. Mamma . . . Babs, I could have loved you if I'd not been afraid of you. You did us more harm than Captain because we had you so long.

I have never cried much, I hate the feeling of tears. I felt the hot sticky feeling of them. I looked at Bonnie, her eyes were like syphons. We cried together for something we'd never had and never would have, we cried for the feelings that we'd never felt.

Babs, our lovely mother, had died alone, without kindness, without hair, teeth or dignity. Downstairs, Bo was shouting at Eden. All Eden's fault, all his sisters' fault, fat cows, bloody curs. I blew my nose.

'Bonnie, we'll have to close her eyes now. You have to do that when they're dead.'

'I'm not touching her. You must be barmy. I'm not doing it. You can.'

My fingers were wet, Babs' face was wet. I couldn't do it, such cold skin, soft yet hard. Her eyelashes might come loose, her eyes might roll out. Mascara had washed into her eye sockets, like particles of grit. I remembered the wedding and her eyes behind the flowery eye veil.

'I think you have to put pennies on them to keep them shut. Get some money.'

'You know we haven't any. Leave it, Tor.'

'What about the window? Irish people open it when people die. To help the soul fly to heaven.'

'There's no glass in the skylight, you must be barmy. She didn't believe in heaven, she's not a peasant. Let's go down now to Bo.'

It didn't seem right to leave her. We looked at the skylight, the air was fresh, the sky was blue. We were orphans.

A blackbird started to sing (they had nested earlier, in the laurels) sounding sweet and clear. Babs would have liked that. Bird song was nicer than harps or angels. Bo was still shrieking down below.

ELEVEN

'Drink your lemon, Dadda. It will do you good.'
'Tell me that she didn't suffer. Tell me again what she said.'
'Nothing, I told you. I don't know what Father said to her.
She went up to the attic, she left us alone.'
Captain lay in a corner bed in the hospital, begging to be reassured. He wanted to believe that Babs hadn't been unhappy. He wanted to know what she'd been thinking and feeling the last time she'd climbed those attic stairs. He clutched at Bo with shaky hands. She'd not suffered, had she?
'There, there, Dadda. I shouldn't think she did. You know what the coroner said. The oul' roof fell on her while she was sleeping. She'd taken pills, of course.'
We were at the hospital after the funeral. The days following the death passed in a daze. Brad had been on the danger list himself when he'd heard the news. His temperature rose, he'd abandoned himself to grief and remorse. Had it been his fault? Had he not spent so much time in Fagin's Bar, would she be with us still? Had Mick encouraged him, to suit his own sinful gain?

I suppose he loved Babs as much as he was capable of loving, and their attic had been his heaven on earth.

The nursing sisters exhorted him with grave faces. Less of the self-pity, Man dear, hadn't he his family to love him? Hadn't he a reason for hope? Hadn't his family wanted him, Man dear?

When we arrived he was drinking lemon squash. He was tearful. He'd wanted to follow her to the grave. He'd had double pneumonia the sisters said, we shouldn't stay too long. Just tell about the funeral and leave. I tried to pity him. This was the officer who had swept Babs off her feet, our military stepfather who had gazed adoringly while champagne corks popped and flew. He cried now, he begged for information; uneasy about Mick Fagin, not asking outright, you could feel it was on his mind. Unspoken anxiety nagged at him, he begged Bo to allay his fears.

Who had taken the service? Tell him she'd not suffered. Who had been there? She'd had a happy life, he'd done his best for her, no one could gainsay it. Who had sent flowers?'

'Drink your lemon, it will do you good.'

They made him drink constantly; cups of Bovril, weak tea, milk with egg in it. Weak drinks for a sorrowing man.

Bo was offhand about the service. His mammy had been a heretic, had died outside the blessing of the true church. We had had to travel to a Protestant graveyard, some miles off, she'd not deserved more. He'd behaved with exaggerated piety, intoning prayers in Latin, fervently kissing his beads. There had been few mourners and few flowers. Bo had his inner sorrow like Bonnie and I, but couldn't show it. After the service was over, the town taxi took us to the hospital. I was glad Captain had a corner bed.

The nursing sisters wore clashing beads hanging from their waistbands as they hastened between the beds. The old man next to the Captain scratched and peered between the sheets. 'There y'are. Got you. There now.' His bony fingers pounced and cracked imaginary insects. He looked at us with a grin.

Captain continued sniffing and questioning. His tears might atone for our own dry eyes, might atone for the parish who hadn't cared. That stuck-up woman from England who attended no service, who showed no neighbourliness, was unmourned (except, so it was whispered, for that one at Fagin's Bar). She had got her just deserts. She would be slandered until the next scandal touched the town; she would be forgotten.

Captain wore an ugly hospital gown that opened at the back. The sisters had given him a shave. They had left a small patch by his ear because of a pimple. I hadn't seen him with pimples before. He had lost weight. Bo clicked his tongue. Drink your lemon, Dadda, don't be making that noise, you'll get a coughing fit. There now. Mammy was very likely in some better place, a paradise for heretics. The skylight fell on her, she'd be with her own kind now. There now, not to cry.

'Surely you heard something, some kind of sound?'

'The roof fell, we heard nothing. Accidental death, the coroner said.'

'Were there many flowers for her?'

'A few flowers, white and rosy ones. Fagin's sent a wreath. I brought a flower from it. See, Dadda. Pink. Smell.'

'Fagin's?'

'Smell.' Rose-smelling, her favourite scent.

'The Grange is a ruin. We're not sleeping there now. We moved.'

Captain picked at the flower. He was unconcerned where we had moved, he was consumed with his own unease. More tears oozed from his lids. His was an unfortunate lot, ruined financially, near death, the light of his life gone. Pink roses, her favourite flower.

I told him that the Grange could be repaired, that it would cost a lot. Eden would help. Moving out had been his idea.

'Debris and disgrace. She said so. I am a ruined man.'

'Yes, well, we've lost our mother, remember. It's been a bad time. Eden has helped.'

'Where is Eden?'

'We came alone. He's coming to see you tomorrow. He wants to talk.'

'Talk? I'm widowed. Ruined. Why does he want to talk?'

Bonnie looked at me. His brain must be affected. Would we have to bear that too? She leaned over the bed with a sweet expression, she put her hand on his.

'Listen, Captain dear, Tor and I have been thinking. From now on we're going to call you Bradwell. It's not as if we're properly related, and you're not a Captain any more, it sounds barmy. Tor and I are grown up. We'll say Bradwell from now on.'

Pretty Bonnie smiled. She looked like Babs. Brad had chased her, had tried to harm her, he had made Babs miserable. He must stay in the hospital until we brought his clothes. New names couldn't make new starts, couldn't bring respect. He was sickening. Was Bonnie losing her tender heart?

He had Bo's love. Bo had got his own way about school. He could write his rhymes, be near his dadda, there would be no more rows. He took the corner of Brad's sheet and wiped his face kindly. There, there, Dadda, not to cry. Say a round of the beads for dear mammy. Smell the flower and pray for her soul.

A nun with a handkerchief the size of a towel came clicking between the beds. What way was this to be carrying on in front of the ward? Shame. Many a sick man here would give a year of his life for a lovely son and daughters to visit and console him. Give thanks to God and his Blessed Mother. Wasn't he alive himself and with a future to live? The sisters would be remembering his family in chapel. Had his wife been a Catholic, he could have had a requiem said. Give thanks, dry those tears.

'Ah, you're very good, Sister,' Brad said in a whining tone.

'You've been quite ill, Brad,' I told him. He must concentrate on getting strong. Eden would repair the Grange roof.

'You don't hold anything against me do you, Tor? Nor you, Bonnie?'

The sister was ringing a bell in the doorway. Time for goodbyes now. She moved towards the man with the scratching fingers. Whiffs of Listerine came from her gown. He plucked my skirt, he whispered that my father had spoken of breeding Guernseys, that he could help there.

Bo climbed onto the bed for a last embrace, the frilled pillow made a frame for their heads. He rubbed against his father's cheek. There, there, no need to fret now. Mammy was in a sort of heaven, a heavenly place for lost souls. She probably had felt nothing when the roof fell. No more tears, drink the lemon.

'Boris, my pal,' Brad moaned.

'When do they bring your tea?' Bo was brisk. He was peckish. He'd relish a little biscuit or a cake with raisins. Don't be crying, when was tea?

I don't remember kissing Bradwell before. He smelled like the nuns' habits as well as wet hankies. At the last moment I pulled back, my kiss turned into a sort of a cough. Bonnie shook his hand, keeping her smile sweet. You never knew with nuns, they might keep him here for years.

Our feet tapped the floor as we left his bed. There were no other visitors. I pushed the swing door. From the other side came the chant of plain song. I looked back; the nun was picking the rose petal from his sheet, straightening his covers, patting his hand. Her lips moved. Give thanks . . . blessings, dry those tears . . . Now what about a smile?

The taxi smelled of chrysanthemums and also of shoe polish. We had done our duty to Brad the sick widower, taken flowers. He could lie and imagine her grave with Fagin's wreath on it. Perhaps Bonnie and I might get closer with our parents out of the way, but there was still Eden. She changed when he was near, looking at him, listening when he spoke, keeping her eyes wide.

The taxi drew up at the Grange gates where he was waiting for us. He'd insisted that we should visit Brad on our own. Tomorrow he would go and discuss plans for the future, as well as the restoration of the Grange.

In a short time he'd worked wonders on the lodge. The windows had glass in them now. While we'd been at the hospital he'd been cutting back the wild rose bush that had spread itself round the door. He wore old dungarees. Branches and suckers lay on the ground, the rain-dampened thorns hadn't yet grown dark and sharp. He'd cleared all the broken glass and rubbish from behind the broken wall. Old tins and rags lay in a heap. He planned to make a small garden, with a path to the door. There was room for a lawn and flower-beds and perhaps a sundial. The rose, properly pruned, might produce proper blooms. But I liked the single ones with dropping petals and pollen that dusted your hands. Eden would make a warm and weatherproof residence for us until the Grange was restored. Bonnie and I had been keen to move to the lodge. We needed a new start after the past weeks in the Grange.

Bo and Eden slept downstairs on mattresses. Bo was in charge of the fire. Eden had given him a lesson in lighting it with sticks. They found some coal behind the lodge. Bonnie and I slept in the loft overhead. There was just room for our mattresses.

The wettest August in memory was over, the sun had shone for Babs' death and each day since. An Indian summer was forecast. Next spring our garden would bloom. Bonnie helped Eden with the clearance and digging, she'd never worked like that before. She planned carnations and asparagus fern. Her favourite was love-in-the-mist.

Soon it felt as if we'd lived in the lodge for ages. It was safe, I didn't want to leave.

Most of Babs' things in the attic were unusable. We went through her jewelry box, making three piles of her trinkets. Bonnie wanted the rings. I divided the brooches and bracelets between me and Ula, but in the end I kept only the watch. I don't like jewelry, but a watch was useful. It was too dainty for a nurse to use. In a drawer, under her necklaces, we found some papers. It seemed Babs had a little money in savings bonds. Bonnie told Eden, who told us to say nothing about it for the time being. A nest-egg never came amiss, we'd learn that one day. It wasn't a lot, we would need money to restore the Grange. I had hoped to find something that showed that Babs had worried about me. She had never said she loved me, or had hopes, or was proud; she never said much at all. She loved Bonnie, pretty Bonnie of the forget-me-not eyes. Once when I'd had a cold she'd give me a juicy pear, smiling at me. She had cut and peeled it, putting the pieces in my hand. The juice trickling down my sore throat was lovely, the gritty softness of pears would remind me of her, now. Her attic clothes smelled of flood water as well as roses. In the hamper was a picture of our real blood father, looking like Ula. I stared, I couldn't remember him. Why couldn't he be here now instead of Bradwell? The savings bonds might be useful one day but we needed money now. Eden had the good idea of selling the cow.

It had stayed in the barn during the worst weather. We'd

always loathed it, time now for it to go. We'd never taken to milking, it was almost dry anyway. It took delight in fouling our shoes or kicking the bucket over. Eden arranged for the Fagin brothers to have it. It was taken off early one morning, we never saw it again.

We had money to settle the Co-op. We wouldn't have to shop at Fagin's any more. We could buy wellingtons and raincoats, clothes for the winter. Bonnie bought lipsticks and eye make up. We threw all Babs' stuff away. The cow would have a better life at the Fagins'; they would put the bull to it and make it calve again. They were used to milking and had a real farm. We were left with Bo's duck.

Bo and I went for walks together, Bonnie didn't want to come now Eden was here. Bo was much happier, though he missed Brad. His scabs and scratches healed, he was calmer, his nightmares stopped, he didn't scratch or bite. I showed him how to pull grass stalks gently, leaving the outer sheath behind to keep the part you sucked clean. He hummed as he sucked, his wellingtons rubbed the backs of his knees leaving red patches. He swiped at dandelions and stirred cow-pats with twigs. He went alone to visit Bradwell, Bonnie and I didn't go again. The hedges bordering the fields smelled hot and a little rotten that summer. Bo still wrote rhymes on scraps of paper. He might turn the Grange into a seminary one day. His plans became wilder as the weeks went by.'

'Yes, well, I want to be a nurse myself. I'm not like Bonnie.'

'Eden is a good chap,' Bo said in a wise voice. He said that what Bonnie needed was to become someone's wife. Or maybe the life of an actress would suit her, as long as no one asked her to sing.

'She's much too young for marriage. Don't be silly, Bo.'

'Don't you be so sure, you may get a surprise.'

'What surprise? What do you mean?' Hadn't we already had enough shocks and surprises this summer?

'I mean Eden.'

'What about him? It's not serious. Bonnie is just flattered that he likes her. That's all. She doesn't love him.'

'Oh doesn't she? She does, the silly cow.'

'You're wrong. You're quite wrong. You're silly.'

I hated him for thinking it about my Bonnie. If she married him she might get a baby. She'd ask me to be bridesmaid and walk behind her, all tricked up in frills and flowers. I wasn't going to be an aunt to anyone, I wasn't that sort. She shouldn't dream of marrying anyone until she was at least thirty. She shouldn't dream of Eden at all.

I remembered the way he watched her, the way he looked at her each time he spoke. He waited on her, he was making a garden of flowers for her. He was even showing her how to cook.

Cooking on an open fire was an art he'd learned at a boys' club. You needed a thick pan with a tight lid. The first cake that Bonnie made was runny in the middle. Eden had laughed tenderly. Bo ate the cake with a spoon. Pancakes were easier, Eden would show her those next time. She'd be the finest cook in the land.

Eden planned to restore the Grange to former glory. He had a book, *Student Guide to Plumbing and Home Maintenance*. It had a section on electrical repairs. He intended to start evening classes with the Christian Brothers, who taught woodwork. Bo wanted to carve religious objects for his altar. There was no time for anyone to become seriously romantic in this family. If Bonnie had any sense she'd learn homecraft to qualify her for earning her living. She might manage a caff, for instance, or become a matron of a school.

I wondered about Ula, I should be with her. She was probably in pain, she was sure to be lonely and worrying about what was going on. In the old days, particularly at boarding school, Bonnie had mothered her. She only seemed to care about Eden now, smiling at him, listening, baking those uneatable cakes. Babs would be shocked at all this. Eden spoke badly, he wasn't well educated, his flattery had stolen Bonnie's wits. Wait, Bonnie, don't be rash; we are different from Eden and people like him. He's kind but he'll never change.

Bo chose another grass stalk, pulling it slowly. We heard it squeak. He said in a mincing tone that he hoped Bonnie knew about sexual intercourse, poor old creature.

'Don't be so rude and crude, Bo. You're always showing off.'

Sex was something we didn't mention. We had found out about it in a dreadful way, on the night our headmistress died at school. Two girls brought soldiers into an empty dormitory. I and my sisters had heard. We crept in and saw a sort of orgy, two under a blanket on the floor, two on a bed. One of the girls was an evacuee from London, the other was our own head girl. We watched without speaking, I felt like fainting. We never mentioned it again. Now here was my little brother talking casually about Bonnie and sex. He smiled in a superior way. I was too prim and priggish, he said. I ought to move with the times.

Bonnie had on her secret expression when we got in again. She'd been experimenting with another cake. You had to line the pot thickly with paper before the mixture went in. The fire must be hot, you had to pile red coals over the lid. When we walked in, we were met by a lovely smell. She had used raisins, nuts, cinnamon and orange peel. It was a perfect cake.'

'Isn't Eden clever? He showed me. We used four eggs.'

Eden smiled for joy. She was wonderful to teach, and so amenable.

'You like Eden showing you things don't you, Bonnie darlin?' Bo leaned over to whisper something. Bonnie tittered. I felt left out. This cake-making was a bad sign. If she wasn't careful she'd be an old woman with ten children and expect me to be godmother. Neither of us could knit properly, we hated it. I wanted my own life, I wanted to be a nurse in a hospital. Besides, what about Ula and Bo?

I liked the attic with Bonnie, with just room to walk round our mattresses and the smell of pears and dust in the corners. We hung our clothes from nails in the rafters. It was like a tree house. I slept well, until the night I heard Bonnie go down. Her feet scuffed the ladder rungs. I didn't hear the back door open; she wasn't going to the lavatory. Was she sleep-walking? I knew she was going to Eden, to learn more of his secrets. She would whisper, perhaps they would kiss.

It was the middle of the night. She had a clean nightdress on. She'd been using some of Babs' scent. What had Babs done with Mick Fagin? Had they met at this lodge? I couldn't hear. I crawled off my mattress to the top of the ladder. I craned my head down. Bonnie and Eden were on the floor by the fire. I saw their shadows. They were sitting crossways, her legs were each side of his, in the shape of a squatting bear. Supposing Bo woke and saw? Bonnie was shameless, she had gone down on purpose, she couldn't get enough of Eden. You are disgusting, Bonnie, you are rude. Eden has stolen your wits. I leaned further. What *was* she doing now?

Then it happened. The animal sound, the pants, the whispers, I heard the same words that I'd heard before. It was the same as that night at school, the same words said by the same voice. 'Stuck up bitch, I'll teach you, like I done Red.' Eden had been one of those soldiers hiding under the blanket in the dormitory. He was saying the same to Bonnie as he'd said to our head girl. He was doing the same thing to Bonnie, my pretty sister. 'Stuck up bitch. I'll teach you.' He was the soldier boyfriend of that evacuee from Clerkenwell, the girl called Red, who smelled sickly. The girl with the sniggering laugh. She had brought soldiers to the dormitory to practise intimacy.

A bitch is a female dog. Not my Bonnie, she is noble and fine, she is mine. 'I'll teach you like I done Red.'

I crouched at the top of the ladder till my body ached. Was this what Babs had done? I didn't want to hear, I had to hear. I would never feel the same again. Too much was happening too fast. Bonnie was . . . 'Stuck up bitch'.

Eden was just an upstart, he was making use of her. He was unforgiveable, he was base, he should be locked up.

Come back, Bonnie.

TWELVE

I must have slept, because I didn't hear her come back. Then I had this dream about finding money. I was in a field in the rain and finding money everywhere. First there was a shilling in a patch of shamrock, then a florin further on. A half-crown glittered under a bramble bush, a ten-shilling note was stuck on a thorn. I stretched my hand out, I called to Bonnie that it was all right, we had money. I felt the thorn prick as I woke. The happy feeling didn't leave me, in spite of the shock earlier. Bonnie was there breathing deeply, everything was all right. Perhaps finding money was a good omen, Ireland might be lucky for us after all. I liked the lodge, I didn't want to go back to England; I had the feeling of belonging here, though I had seen nothing of Ireland except this place, and met few of the people. If only Bonnie hadn't spoiled things, I wanted to shout at her, hit her. I saw. I heard. I know.

Eden was frying sausages on a spirit lamp bought from the Co-op. Bo was trying to light the fire. The lodge fireplace was bigger than the Grange one. He blew the sparks busily, the room was smokey. Bo didn't bother to steal money now. Eden looked calm and cheerful, my own face was the shamed red one. I wanted to hit him with his frying pan. I saw. I heard. I know. You only care about pleasing Bonnie, you're plotting to capture her, you don't think about Bo or me. Your sausages smell disgusting, you are disgusting, give them to Bonnie, she won't say no. She's upstairs asleep with her mouth open, her hair is straggly round her cheeks that are soft as a rose. Did you kiss her mouth, her hair and her cheeks, Eden? Where else did you kiss?

'Here she is. Did you sleep well, Bonnie?'

'Sausages? I'm starved. What shall we do today, Eden?'

'I thought we'd carry on with the garden.'

'Lots of love-in-the-mist,' she said wistfully.

'What about love-lies-bleeding?' I said.

Bo thought that a garden without flowers was best, with room to play. A garden of bubbles, that's what he'd like. Many sizes, many colours, freely floating, filling the air.

I left them talking about the garden. I went up again to enter my diary. I would never forget that squatting bear. I saw. I heard. I know.

'I can't think why you bother with that diary still. You should have outgrown it by now.' Bonnie made a grab at it, she started reading it.

'Saw what? Heard what? Know what?'

My throat felt like dry bread. 'Don't do it, Bonnie. He's not the person you think he is. He's . . . he's . . . '

'Yes? Who is he? What?'

'He's that soldier. That night at school. Under the blanket. That Christmas. He's the boyfriend of that girl called Red. His name is Ed, he isn't Eden . . . '

'As a matter of fact, for your information, I do know. I know everything. He *used* to be called Ed. He *used* to be Red's boyfriend, that's all over. He's Eden now. In any case how do *you* know?'

'I heard. I couldn't help hearing. I heard what he said. The same as that night, that Christmas when we saw.'

'You mean you eavesdropped? You snooped and sneaked. I might have known.'

'I had to, Bonnie. Don't say that. I had to know.'

'You needn't worry. Eden and I have no secrets. We tell everything.'

'How could you? With *him*. He's that soldier.'

The girls had jostled to look at Eden's photograph, only then he had been Ed. Red, the evacuee from Clerkenwell, was only thirteen. She had a vulgar laugh, she smelled of dirt and vanilla essence and was loved by the soldier called Ed. His face, clean-shaven and gap-toothed, had grinned from the frame. He wore a tank beret over stubbly hair. He had written ITALY in the corner, a secret love-code. Ed had taught Red how to dance. Now he made eyes at Bonnie, having changed to Eden. It was disgusting. I saw. I heard. I know.

She told me I was barmy to make such a fuss. Eden was her lifeline, he meant the world to her, as she did to him. He couldn't get enough of her, he'd said so. And just think how kind he was.

'Yes. I see why, now. He's using you. You're a convenience. Can't you see?'

Bonnie's voice changed when she spoke of him. It all sounded so greedy, as if she were a plate of food. He was making use of her.

'We're using each other. You don't understand, Tor, you're too young.'

I understood all right, I saw the truth. She was just thinking of herself.

'I must, Tor. No one else will. I'm not like you. I'm not interested in training. I've got to get away. I just want Eden.'

'And Ula? What about her?'

She said that Brad was Ula's guardian. Perhaps when she and Eden had settled they would send for her. She didn't sound concerned.

'You mean you'll leave the Grange?'

When we were little we used to play with imaginary children. Bonnie's were called 'Marigold' and 'Delphine'. My baby was black. She beat her two with coat-hangers and locked them under the stairs. She had the same coat-hanger-beating look in her eyes.

'You don't expect me to stay here? What is to keep me?'

'I'm beginning to like it. I want to be a nurse, but I'll want to come back. I don't know why.'

'Eden is going to teach me dancing. Proper dancing. We'll have a flat and a garden full of flowers.'

'When?'

She closed her eyes, swaying romantically. I asked too many questions. Eden would arrange everything. He'd won medals at ballroom. As a professional, she'd partner him.

I imagined her dancing in his arms, round their home and into their garden of flowers. They would travel to far off lands and win contests.

'He isn't like us, Bonnie. Do be careful. Babs wouldn't have approved at all.'

'*Babs*? What has she to do with it? I don't suppose she'd care.'

'She wouldn't like it. Do you ever miss her?'

I thought of the times I had stood on the landing listening to her and Babs talking about clothes, doing exercises, in a private world. Bonnie, the bridesmaid, the one who got watches and pearl rings, the first to hear about Bo, the first to hold him when he was born.

'I can't think of the past. I have Eden.'

'Don't change too much.' She still had a family. Would she forget us?

'I know what I'm doing. Eden is wonderful. He's going to buy me a silk dress for dancing. I'll have sandals with gold straps.'

'You won't go having a baby, will you? It could happen.'

'Oh could it? And how do you know, snooper?'

'I couldn't help hearing. He's using you. You're just a stepping stone. Don't forget, he comes from the slums.'

'At least I'm not a snob, Tor. You're worse than Babs. You're jealous, aren't you?'

'No I'm not. Of course I'm not. But he's a pretender, he isn't real. The way he speaks isn't real. Haven't you noticed?'

'What's wrong with change? What's wrong with trying to improve? He hated his old life. He wants me.'

'Don't you mind about Red? Don't you care? It's horrible.'

'It's not. It's over, past. Dead. He's mine now. He's changed and I've changed. I'm dying to learn to dance.'

It sickened me to think of her in Red's trashy wake. Red of the thin red lips and coarse talk, Red of the bitten nails and tin rings. She'd had experience with boys. She had an influence on the school. The girls had watched and copied her. She had taught us to frizz our hair. Because of her, nail polish had spilled over our school blouses. Because of her, we knew the Lambeth Walk. Life in her Clerkenwell sounded jolly and noisy, never lonely.

You couldn't compare Bonnie with Red. My Bonnie was sublime as well as noble. She hummed and swayed round her mattress, with a pillow clutched to her chest. She knew about real kissing now. Pretty Bonnie, stay as you were.

Bo's head appeared at the top of our ladder. A party? He'd join us with the duck. And then we were dancing in a ring round the mattresses; we waved our arms, we joined in Bonnie's song. Bo imitated her terrible voice. Happiness was hard to catch, it dissolved in your hands so easily, floating, alighting, bubble-frail.

'Don't look so serious, Tor.'

'Don't do anything rash will you, Bonnie?'

'What are you talking about? Who is rash?' A rasher of

bacon was what Bo would relish. He didn't like sausages so well. Who was rash?

'Shut up, the two of you. And take the duck off my bed.'

I knew she would go creeping down again tonight, smelling of roses, to learn more of the secrets of life. Their limbs would entwine, they'd hug and whisper. Once you started, you had to go on until you'd learned all you could learn. You didn't think about the consequences, only your own need.

I thought I could hinder her by staying up late. I would sit by the fire and spoil their privacy. I would keep an eye on her, as Babs should have done. Though the lodge was only two rooms and we had no privacy, I felt secure now. Eden mustn't spoil it. Bonnie must be chaperoned. Baking cakes and dreaming of dancing was one thing, running off with an impostor, another.

'Go to bed, Tor. Stop yawning.'

'Poor old soul, little Tor is worn out.' Bo picked up one of Babs' magazines with pictures of models with long legs and thrusting bosoms. Their eyes were like Bonnie's, watching and waiting.

'Go on, Tor. You're dead beat.'

The lodge lavatory was a small shed at the back with a broken door. You had to hold the string tied to the latch, but even that was better than the Grange. The board with a hole in it over a drain wasn't comfortable. Small animals rustled in the undergrowth outside. I would stay out there as long as possible, put a stop to Bonnie's behaviour. A spider caught the light from my torch, motionless, watching and waiting. Insects had never frightened us, we used to play with them, cradling them in hankies and matchboxes, christening them, racing them, fondling them. Woodlice were best. Don't do it, Bonnie. He isn't right.

Something large was snuffling and scratching outside the door, a badger or a fox perhaps. A little boney-legged hedge hog was scuttling through the weeds. Its black-tipped spines looked so charming, the fur framed its eyes like a flattened moustache. I would have liked to have caught it, I would like it as a pet, to put insects in the way of its routing snout, to give it a happy home.

'Stop fussing over it, Tor. They're vermin. They're flea-ridden. Go to bed.'

I made the old meat-safe into a nest for it. I got a cushion, I put out a saucer of milk.

The dish was licked clean in the morning, the cushion in the meat-safe looked dented, but I never saw it again. Eden said that hedgehogs were the gardener's friend, ridding the flowers of slugs and snails. Would it sniff round the roots of his love-in-the-mist? Would its fleas bite Bonnie's limbs? Searching and wondering about it kept my mind off her. What I dreaded most was that she'd have a child.

THIRTEEN

The Indian summer continued, the hot dry days passing slowly and lazily. Brad was still in the hospital under the care of the sisters, I still loved the lodge. It was like living in a dolls' house. We were two couples, Eden and Bonnie, Bo and I. There were no irksome chores, Eden cooked lovely food. We sunbathed in front of the lodge, we walked in the fields, sucking grasses and singing songs.

Each morning we ate our porridge outside in the morning dew. A donkey brayed far off. It wasn't the Ireland of fiction or expectation. It was the quiet that I loved, the little wild flowers, the fuchsia in the hedges outside the gate, the straight road that stretched to the town. Bo was fatter and more gentle.

The day that the letter came, he and I were watching Bonnie picking roses. I sat on the wall. Bo was licking his bowl. The duck was by Bonnie's feet. Once they were picked, the petals fell quickly, pollen fell on her bare toes. Bo was to start at the Brothers' school in a fortnight. My own future wasn't settled, but I'd written for information about nursing. The sun was hot on my head.

Bonnie knew she looked beautiful, stretching up to the

roses. Her shirt colour was the same colour as the sky and the flowers. Eden was at the back clearing the growth round the lavatory; he'd make a path before the winter, so that we'd keep dry. Restoring the Grange was a long-term project, he'd make the lodge comfortable first. I looked forward to the winter. The less I worried about Bonnie the better; she was adult, she must look after herself. I had written to Ula about Babs dying. England seemed another world; poor little Ula, she hadn't answered yet. The postman was late. I watched the duck picking round Bonnie's feet. I will think of Ula and ducks and hedgehogs. The postman may have a letter from her. Bonnie was sick this morning. Her period is five days late.

Eden was a man of worth and integrity, the way he worked proved that, but not the man for my sister. Why didn't he speak of his past, was he running from something? He and Bonnie meet each night, I can't stop her. I will think about becoming a nurse.

I love buttercups and dandelions, yellow for sunshine; ducklings, yellow for egg yolk and champagne. Yellow for vomit, sick faces, bile, yellow for despair. I wondered if Eden had found any stolen money. Bo had stopped stealing and Brad was safe.

How long will he stay sober when he comes home again? There isn't room here, could he stay at the Grange? I love this peace, this green and sunshine, the serenity of this life. I want time to stand still, for nothing to happen to Bonnie, for things to stay as they are.

I tried to see Ula's and my own future. I could specialize in orthopaedic nursing and look after her, we could live here in peace and prosperity. She and I would survive. Bo would thrive with the Brothers, he was intelligent, he loved his father. If only I could wave a wand and make Bonnie a virgin again.

'There's the postman. Look, there's his bike, I see him.'

Against the pink sky, far down the road, he was pedalling slowly, his sack limply hanging on his back. He reached the gates, he dismounted, pausing, staring. The lodge had changed. Smoke came from the chimney, the windows had glass, the front was cleared, there were flowerbeds, there was a table with plates on it. Bonnie, lovely in pink, posed with flowers in her hands.

'Hullo,' she said in a throaty voice.

He stared with brown pop-eyes. Had it been him who had gossiped abouts Babs and Mick Fagin? Don't think about that, Babs is dead. I wanted to warn the postman not to idolize her. Bonnie was not what she seemed, she was vain and wild, loose in her ways. Eden had stared like that when he saw her blowing bubbles, look what happened. Turn your eyes away.

She would arrange herself fetchingly on her deathbed for the undertaker, a natural seducer of men. Why should she feel the need to conquer if she was Eden's girl? Just you wait, Bonnie, until you find yourself crooning lullabies with your awful voice. You'll be tired, you'll be tied, the cost of motherhood is high.

'Hullo,' she said, going to the gate. 'We've changed our residence. Isn't it sweet? We live here now.'

The letter wasn't from Ula. It was addressed to Eden.

He came from the back, he rested his rake against the wall. He took the letter, not speaking, not opening it. He put it in his jacket, hanging over the wall. Love made people secretive, he and Bonnie had their sealed world. Why should he hide the letter from her? He could be a murderer or a bigamist. Why didn't he ask her to marry him instead of filling her head with dreams of dancing and gardens? He should be planning wedding bells, diamond rings and champagne.

We weren't an ordinary family, we never would be. We were too sensitive, took life too much to heart. We might not succeed in what we tried, but we must try. Bo would soon be an ordinary school boy at a local school, I had my nursing plan. All Bonnie seemed to do was stare at her stomach with a fixed look, or smile into Eden's eyes.

If there was a child there, it would blight her. She wasn't suited to becoming a teenage mamma. She should be eating oranges and fish oil instead of stuffing silly cakes and posing with roses. Squatting like a bear with Eden each night might amuse her, it didn't amuse me at all. Bonnie, don't have a child, have a period.

She'd always been like clockwork, never suffered from cramps or headaches like me, never bled for more than four days, could time her first drop of blood almost to the minute. Spots, greasy hair or nasty feet never bothered Bonnie. But now she'd lost her common sense. She would need special clothes if she were pregnant. She would swell and her milk would drip. She needed cash and a wedding at once, this week. What was Eden doing about it?

The letter could be about plans for their future, it might have money in it. Perhaps I misjudged him, he might be planning a home in England where he could establish a wife. If Bonnie was about to give birth, she ought to do it in style. Be proud, pretty Bonnie, and don't expect me to deliver it or sing to it. I don't like motherhood. If it's a girl don't call it some dainty name like Marigold, just teach it to be tough. Love it. Meanwhile what about calcium and vitamins? Stop staring at your stomach, stop eating cake and kissing Eden. My old soul is getting tired.

'Good news, Eden, I hope? Nice little letter?' Bo could be as sweet as Bonnie when he liked.

Eden twitched his fingers. His moustache looked stiff as wire in the morning light. If the letter was about money or jobs he'd open it. It was cruel not to tell Bonnie, she looked unhappy. He should be holding her hand, showing her his letter. She fiddled with her flowers, with the hand that should be wearing a ring. She put the flowers down and went up to the loft.

'Well, aren't you going to read it, Eden?'

He scowled, he took his rake and went to the back again.

'Bo, I'm sure Eden is up to something. He doesn't want anyone to see his letter. I think we should find out. We must read it.'

'Ah me, Tor. No.'

'Ah me, yes. It's our duty. We must read it for Bonnie's sake.'

'He'd kill us.'

'I'm going to look. Go on, your fingers are quick.'

Cunning was in Bo's blood. He slit the envelope silently. I filled the kettle from the outhouse tap. We might need steam for re-sealing. There was Eden by the lavatory, digging, with his back to the lodge. The undergrowth was cleared, the hedgehog would be unprotected. Had he thrown the meat-safe away?

'Tor. Come here. Listen to this.

> 'Dear Ed. Long time no see no hear. I heard you was in Ireland I'm still fancy free. Mum has our little boy, he wants his Dad now. Don't forget our arrangement long time no see or hear love Red.'

Who is it? Who is Red?'

'Hush. Keep your voice down. Don't let Bonnie hear. Red is . . . It's awful.'

'Who is she? Who?'

'It's Eden's old girl-friend. He used to be called Ed.'

'Did he tell you? Who is she?'

'We knew her once. Not Eden. She was evacuated to our school, ages ago. Before you were born. Don't let Bonnie hear.'

'You never told me, you never said. What does it mean "Our little boy?" This Red and Eden must have some secret child.' Ah me. Ah tangled love.

'It's a . . . disaster. Eden isn't right for Bonnie. I said he wasn't. It's a disgrace.'

'Poor, dear little Bonnie.'

'Keep your voice down. It's the worst thing that has ever happened.' My Bonnie. Did Red want Eden back?

She might even be married to him. Pretty Bonnie, where are you now? You ran twice to the lavatory this morning, I heard you. Being sick is a sign of a child. It's no good hoping it won't happen, I think it has.

'Quickly. Put it back. He's coming.'

Re-seal the envelope, put it in his jacket. Eden is banging the back door. Now he's running the tap over his hands. Will he notice the paper is torn?

Bo and I stood in the doorway, not looking at him. We heard the envelope crackle, heard it being crushed in his hand.

'Everything all right, Eden?' Bo's voice was full of concern.

Eden cleared his throat. He flicked his hair back.

'Listen, kids. I got to . . . I have to leave. To London, actually. Right away, 's'matter of fact.'

'Oh dear. Why, Eden?'

'Something come up . . . came up. A bit of business. Where is Bonnie?'

'Here I am. Up here.'

Her sandals appeared at the top of the ladder, her tanned legs and her shorts. She looked ill. She had heard Bo reading the letter. I was afraid she'd be sick again. She kept swallowing, Eden's pink shirt accentuated her pale colour, a petal had caught in her hair. Now, Bonnie, the time has come to assert yourself. Be proud, demand your rights. Insist on reading that letter, ask what it means. Eden hasn't told you everything, he'd hiding something. Be tough.

'Must you go, Eden. I don't think Bonnie is well. Don't go.'

'You never said, Bonnie. Not well, dear? What's up? I won't be gone long. It's . . . business. Will you be all right?'

She nodded.

Another time she must come with him, he said. She'd be better resting at present. If she felt poorly the crossing might not agree with her. Rest. Take it easy. All right?

The way her hands dangled and her eyes begged made me angry. Stop being humble, Bonnie, take a stand. Fall in a fit, threaten him, slap him. But she said nothing.

'Must you go, Eden? Is it absolutely necessary?'

He looked irritated as he answered me. Unfortunately, yes.

Was he already longing for Red's scrawny arms waiting to grab him? Would they lurk in Clerkenwell doorways? Would he sniff her vanilla and dirt? She must have power over him, her letter was a magnet. Pretty Bonnie came second, Red wanted him, Red came first. He had taught her to tango, dipping and darting round cheap dance halls. Who will teach Bonnie the hesitation waltz?

He left the next day for the night boat to Liverpool. Bonnie even helped him to pack. We leaned over the lower half of the door watching him leave us, his raincoat over his arm. He was thinner now and browner than when he'd first come. Loving Bonnie had improved his looks. If she'd had more experience he might have ignored that letter. Bonnie had given him too much too quickly. She'd had no practice, having had few men in our lives.

Bo waved him off importantly. 'Have no fear, Eden. I'll mind the ladies while you're gone.'

We watched until he was a tiny figure down the road. We were three on our own again.

'Bonnie darlin', you'll be the blushing bride yet. Don't despair, you'll walk down the aisle on my arm.'

'Shut your mouth, Bo, don't tease her. Can't you see how Bonnie feels?'

Bo said he knew a lot more than we thought. Who could make fires burn? Who brought the coal in? We'd miss him if he wasn't around. It would be as well if he slept up in the loft tonight, in case we got afraid in the night.

'I'm not having you near me, you little Irish rat, or your duck either.' Bonnie spoke with venom, but her face looked better. Nothing stopped Bo, he was irrepressible. He started inventing a rhyme. He walked round the table chanting. 'I'm forever blowing bubbles, sister Bonnie lost her man, stole her heart away, leaving her to . . . '

'Oy oy. Anyone at home?'

Silhouetted against the evening sky was a young woman with frizzed hair. She had thin lips, a spotty neck. Her small eyes peered through her fringe.

'Red.' I would know her anywhere.

'Tor and Bonnie. I sort of guessed. Where's Ed?'

'Why are you here, Red?'

Bonnie's face was flushed, she jumped up, agitated.

'I'd had an idea we'd meet one day. Long time no see, Bonnie.'

'Why are you here? Eden left today. He's not here, he went to London.'

'He got my letter, then? He done well for hisself I must say, living in a Grange. Is this it?'

Bo unbolted the door for her, bowed over her hand. In the absence of his father, he was her host. A thousand welcomes to Ireland and to the Grange.

'You their brother? Bit small for a Grange.'

Bo explained. He was Boris. We'd had a flood. His father was ill, so was Ula. He was in charge. Red must look on the lodge as her home.

'Bo, what are you saying?'

'I mean it, Tor. Red is welcome. She has come a long way.'

'I'll stop for tonight. Pity I missed Ed. What happened to your mum?'

For a moment I saw the lodge through Red's eyes; small, bare, poor. But I had been happy here, especially outside, in spite of Bonnie. I didn't want Red to sneer. In spite of the trouble, death and worrying about Bonnie, it was a happy summer.

She stared at Bo's duck. She wasn't keen on birds, feathered things got on her nerves. She'd come on the off-chance, looking for Eden. The pub in the town told her the way.

FOURTEEN

The way she spoke was unforgettable; her stare, her nasal whine, were the same. She seemed even thinner, without bust, stomach or calves, thinner than any of us. Her bitten nails matched her velvet dress and the satchel hanging from her arm. She walked with a little lurch, almost like a dance, because of a broken high-heel. She had no coat or luggage. What had Eden seen in her? I looked at my Bonnie of the beautiful eyes and figure. Red said she was out of cigarettes.

She said if she had the choice she'd stop on at the Grange, no matter how flooded. This lodge wasn't much. And fancy letting that duck on the table. Ducks lived in filth, they got on her nerves. She wasn't keen on animals at all, excepting for her dog. Bo said he loved the duck.

'That all the animals you got, then? Thought you was supposed to have a farm?'

'Did Eden write? How did you know?'

'Course he did. Where's all the animals? Ain't you even got a dog?'

Bo explained about the Grange. Empty for years, then flooded and spoiled. About the cow that was gone. How we were short of funds, temporarily, of course.

Red nodded. Right, she'd caught on. What went wrong? Where was our parents?

'My father is in hospital. Double pneumonia with complications. I am the only son.'

'He drinks,' I told her.

'Right. Shame.'

'He's rather a bad case.'

I didn't care if I upset Bo. I liked telling her. It was like a revenge. Brad didn't deserve loyalty.

'My dad's a boozer. Doesn't do to make too much of it.' If not that, it would be something else, men being what they were. Her dad used to blacken her mum's eyes, bust her nose once, when he was wild. He'd calmed down since he got older.

'Did she mind?'

'Takes a lot to upset my family. I never forgot you, specially Bonnie.'

'And I remember you, Red.'

She said that the school was a right load of toffee noses. Did we ever hear from that head girl?

I didn't answer. I couldn't bear to think of that night of the orgy. ('I'll teach you, like I done Red.')

She was contemptuous about our clothes. We looked bloody poverty stricken, our sandals had seen better days. Bonnie flushed again, we liked the way we dressed. We liked sun and a simple life.

'Simple is right. You don't seem so good, Bonnie. You poorly or something?'

'Of course I'm not.'

I remembered how sick she'd been this morning. Morning sickness could last all day. I knew she was pregnant.

Red sat down, she took her broken shoe off, flexing and rubbing her toes. She had a chain anklet. She said it was a shame about Ula being so poorly. What about our mum?

'She's dead. Didn't you know? Didn't Eden write about it?'

115

'Go on. Never? Dead?'

'We never settled. Our mother (we call her Babs) . . . never settled. She hated Brad drinking.'

'You mean she done herself in?'

'Of course she didn't. The roof fell on her.'

'Oh, right. That's really a shame. You don't seem too upset. If it was my mum, I'd die too.'

'It was upsetting. Very upsetting. Eden was a tremendous help.'

'Course I never had no posh family. Governesses and that, but we got our feelings. I think the world of my mum.'

'Eden is rebuilding the Grange. It will take time.'

'Is he now?'

Bonnie told her that we did miss Babs in our own way. Her death was horrible.

Bo wanted to hear about Red's mother. Never mind now about our mammy, talk about Clerkenwell.

'Mum is all right. I think the world of her. She's got my little boy.'

'Aha.' Bo leaned forward eagerly.

Red's world was another planet, enthralling as a film or play. I remembered the stories she'd told us at school. She'd missed her mum then, the market on a Saturday, jellied eels and chips. I loved the sound of their parlour, the shiny coal scuttle, the fur rug before the fire, the dog called Bones. Her parents drank beer, sometimes her dad became wild. Red and her mum had no secrets, thick as thieves they were. She didn't want to change, she loved Clerkenwell, she didn't want to leave. She'd never forgotten that school of ours.

Bo lent, his elbows on his knees. He did admire her.

'I like your hair. Is Red your real name?'

'Ethelreda. Red to my mates. I always wear red, you might have observed. Me and Ed were a team, won the Saturday spots regular; my best partner, was Ed. You mean you let that duck on the bed?'

'Duck relishes a little comfort.'

'Who sleeps up there?'

'Tor and Bonnie. I sleep down here with Eden. I mean Ed.'

Red sniffed. She said Ireland was a right dead-alive hole.

'Stay, Red. You'll like it. I'm starting with the Christian Brothers. My sisters aren't Catholic, though.'

'You watch them, kiddo. Those Brothers will sour your brains.'

She said she didn't encourage religion in anyone, she never fancied prayers. You had to make things happen, not sit waiting and praying. Dead quiet, this place was. How did we pass our time?

'I like reading. I'll probably be a nurse soon and look after Ula. Bo likes religion and writing rhymes. He had his own altar at the Grange.

'What about Bonn here?'

'She makes cakes don't you, Bonnie? She likes arranging flowers. She wants a garden.'

Our pastimes sounded boring and limited. I added that I liked animals too, I might even be a vet as well as a nurse. We'd not had experience of animals, though Bonnie once had some mice that were killed during the war.

'What do you do for laughs? Have you seen the latest Fred and Ginge picture?'

We never went to films. Red knew the ups and downs of all the stars, all their romances. She could chain-smoke, drink beer, dance the rumba. She was an experienced poker player as well as knowing about boyfriends and what they did. She knew the words of all the popular songs. She yawned. She'd be bored stiff if she had to stop. Some of her back teeth were decayed, her tongue was thin, pointed, a yellowish shade. What in others might be unattractive, was acceptable in Red. She had style.

Bonnie spoke. Did Red remember teaching the school to

do the Lambeth Walk? Those long ago winter nights were safe to remember. Bonnie's present and future were uneasy.

'That's not all I taught you. You were an ignorant lot till us evacuees came. How old was your mum when she passed on?'

'Not old. She couldn't bear this place.'

'It was the skylight. The flood blew it onto her head,' Bo said.

'It was Brad's drinking,' I said.

'Can't say I blame her hating here. A shocking shock though. She must have slept heavy. Luckily you're four of a family, you got each other still.'

'True, Red. Very true.' Bo sighed. Ah me.

Red herself only wanted one child, being an only herself. How was Ed in himself?

'He's restoring and rebuilding the Grange, I told you. Ireland's his home now, he's employed by Brad,' I said firmly.

'Oh, right. We'll have to see about that. I'll have to look at this Grange. I wouldn't mind living somewhere posh for a while. A holiday like.'

'No one can live there. It's uninhabitable.'

'What's up with old Bonn? You look a right miserable misery.'

'It's no wonder. Bonnie is having a child.' The words popped out before I could stop them.

'Shut up, Tor. It's not true. It's nothing to do with you. Shut up.'

Bonnie was frantic. Bo danced about with delight, his rat's face bright with smiles. His little Bonnie with a child in her? Fertilized like a flower? Was Ed the bumble bee? He'd be an uncle. He crossed his arms, flapping his hands. Sister Bonnie with a child. Ah glory me.

'Can't say I'm surprised. Ed's kid, of course? He don't change. Why didn't you say?'

'Why should I? It's no one's business. It is Eden's actually, if you must know. Yes.'

I felt sadder for Bonnie than I could bear. Bo picked up two knives. Bonnie must knit for the babby, he clicked the knives, knit-knit-knit. He'd make up a poem for the birth.

'Silly bitch.'

'So you see, Red, she'll have to marry Eden. She can't have a child on her own.'

'She can't, can't she? Why can't she?'

'It's different for us. She isn't like you, Red.'

'It's different is it? I'll tell you what's different. Ed is mine. We got our arrangement, we made it years back. He belongs to me. He's mine.'

'What arrangement?'

'Arrangement to settle when the time came. To settle somewhere when the time was right. The "when" is now. My little boy needs a dad. Right?'

'You mean you'll marry?'

'Might do. The point is our arrangement. I need him, so does my boy.'

'But what about Bonnie?'

'She'll have to manage, won't she?'

'But Eden and she . . . they . . .'

'Ed would never settle permanent, old Bonn's not his type, not deep down. You're none of you like us.'

'She needs him.'

'I need him more.'

Bo asked why now, especially. Her boy had been all right without Ed until now. Red said she wanted to take up dancing again, she wouldn't mind turning pro. Which meant practice, right? For which she needed Ed. Red and Ed, back in harness, old time partners in the dance.

'Red . . . Ethelreda, can you show me the rumba? I'd relish a little display.'

'Later, kiddo. Wish someone had a fag.'

'There's some of Bonnie's cake.'

'Sod cake, I need a smoke.'

'Watch me, Red. Is this right?' Bo pranced round the table waving his hands.

'Astaire had nothing on you, kid. The thing is, Bonn, you only think you want Ed. You're scared. Right? He'd soon get on your nerves.'

Bonnie's words ran together, her cheeks went a hectic red. Red didn't realize that Eden *wanted* to change, he *wanted* to forget his past. He wanted a different world. He looked different, he spoke differently. She wouldn't know him now.

'Yeah? He always had high ideas. Inside he's weak. He always needs someone to copy. He needs to lean, he doesn't take the lead. It's not accents or manners that counts. Besides, I need him for my partner. Ed and Red.'

'But he loves Bonnie.'

'Love? I know Ed. I'm sure he does.'

'Tor is right. He adores me. We're made for each other. He said.'

'He can adore anyone he likes far as I'm concerned. Only, he's mine.'

'But the baby, don't forget that, Red.'

'She can have it or don't have it, it's up to her. Trouble is, you none of you got no fight.'

'It's different for you, Red. You're not blue-blooded.'

'Blue-blooded? You mean snobs. You're used to the easy life. You flop when things get rough. You're leaners too. Ed's weak but he's mine. I know him. Right?'

'What do you expect Bonnie to do? She'll ruin her life.'

'Want my advice? Get rid of it. Forget it happened.'

'It's dangerous, Red. It's illegal. How?'

Tears came into Bonnie's eyes. Eden wouldn't allow it. Not their child.

'Ed? Wouldn't he? Have you asked him?'

'But how?'

Bo paused in his rumba practice, busily thinking up a rhyme for the occasion.

'Changing partners in the dance, Red and Bonnie share romance.'

Bonnie looked at him with hatred, tears still on her cheeks.

'You and your silly rhymes. I'm sick of you, do you hear?'

'Leave the kid alone. What you need now is cash.'

'We haven't any.' Eden was cashing Babs' bonds for us, the money hadn't arrived.

'I can see that. Poverty stricken.'

Red would get Ed to send some. Quicker the better. The operation was best. Get rid of it. Start fresh.

'Isn't there another way? Where would Bonnie go?'

London was the quickest and best. There were other ways, Red said, but not so certain. You could drink gin in the bath tub, you could jump off tables or swallow quinine. You could shove a knitting needle up you. A special doctor was best. For which you needed cash. Leave it to her, she'd get Ed to send some back, quick as possible.

'I've been feeling so sick, Red.'

'Yeah? Right. Stop feeling sorry for yourself.' Red poked round the lodge. Could she see up in the loft? Fancy sleeping on the floor. She liked the smell of pears. Bo and I stayed downstairs. We got out the cake. We didn't speak. He beat the two knives on the table and tried his rumba step.

Red said the lodge could be all right if it was furnished. She and Bonnie had stayed up the ladder a long time. We heard Red's snickering laugh. They smelled of Babs' scent when they came down. Red wore a pair of Bonnie's shoes. She wondered if our mum's ghost was about in the Grange. She and Bonnie would go there after tea. And what about this altar of Bo's?

After we'd eaten the cake, Bo and I watched them walk

along the drive together. We couldn't hear what they said. Bonnie had her spongebag and two towels over her arm. Red fancied a bath.

FIFTEEN

Rain soaked his hair, ran down his forehead, splashing from his ears and chin. His trouser hems were soaked. The sting of the rain on his roughened hands took his mind off his grief. He stood straight-backed and dripping, watching the funeral.

The mourners and their umbrellas were grouped round the grave. Mud was trickling into the newly-piled earth. It looked shadowy, like the ending of a film. It mustn't end, not yet. A mourner sneezed, a bus swished past outside the wall. Rain from the church guttering overflowed. He had helped staunch the wet before, he could do nothing now. If it could be a film, he could watch it again, could watch her standing on the lawn, thin and lovely, reaching to the bubbles in the sun. A family in Ireland, in a garden, inviting him to stay. Now it was over, he was outside again.

He should be the chief mourner, he'd been the chief love of the deceased, had known her intimately. They were made for each other. But no glances of comfort came his way, no friendly handshakes or pats. He was disgraced. Rain and damp weather would always remind him of Ireland, but this was England now, and Bonnie was dead.

Rain seemed to wash the colour out, even the grass looked the colour of graves.

There was Tor, standing where he should be, her face in her hanky. Someone held an umbrella from behind. That must be Ula at her side, white and ill-looking in a leg-iron. No sign of Bo or Brad. Bo must be heart-broken. Was he in Ireland with his father? Was he tending the fire in the lodge? Tor and Ula, look at me, I want to be part of you. Don't keep me out, I am bereaved.

The moment was coming, the coffin was being lowered, his lovely one was on her way. He wanted to shout out. Stop! No! Don't do it. He was guilty, but they were too. They were in it together. Stop. Don't. He was apart, stick-necked in the rain, while they wept together. The wet ropes slid through the coffin bearers' hands. Their knuckles glistened, the ropes slackened, she was out of sight without a goodbye. Don't go, Bonnie, my dear one. I need you, you are my reason for living, all I desire. My heart and soul, I trusted and loved you. Don't go, Bonnie, be my guide. Your thighs, your breasts, your hair under my fingers are part of me. I can't bear it. I'm part of you. I see you reaching for bubbles, I hear your voice singing. Girl on the lawn, don't go. I'm here.

He must speak to Tor, must explain to her. He'd only wanted to help. The money from the bonds was nothing, he'd wanted money quickly, had gone back on the buses for Bonnie's sake. He'd saved, he'd scraped, couldn't get money fast enough, had taken too much, often, from his day's takings. Because of her he'd thrown caution to the winds. His sentence was harsh, but he'd asked for it. He'd done it for Bonnie's sake. Now, tethered like an animal, he couldn't help no one, not even himself. He stepped forward, was pulled back sharply, he felt the grip of the cuff on his wrist. He couldn't walk to the graveside of his dear one. A common prisoner detained at His Majesty's pleasure, he couldn't even wipe his tears. He needed a handkerchief, his face was wet, his right hand wasn't free. He felt like choking, his hanky was in the wrong pocket, he was trapped. Tor and Ula, look at me, can't you see?

'Here you are, Mack.' The man at his side handed him his own hanky, freshly ironed, still in its square. Ed took it, breathing the smell of it, starched linen, product of loving care. He mopped and blew, nodding his thanks to the jailer who smiled at him.

He could afford a smile, he had a home somewhere, Pentonville most likely supplied comfortable quarters for wives and families. This screw had a wife to love and tend him. Bonnie, dear, I intended to find a real home for you, I wanted to sort something out. I'm your love, your intended bridegroom, you did believe that, didn't you?

No flowers from him, no carnations or love-in-the-mist. The coffin had white flowers as it went down. The priest prayed inaudibly. Bonnie disliked prayers and priests, no one had consulted him about the service. He must go back now to his prison cell.

He saw Tor put away her hanky, turn to her sister in the leg-iron, putting her arms round her, kissing her. Tor, speak, don't leave without a word. You trusted me once, you relied on me. I made the lodge fit to live in for those happy summer days. I am still reliable, still mean to help you. I am loyal, I will stay true, I'll never change. I ran risks for Bonnie's sake, I stole for her and got nicked. I'll be out again, I'll come back to you, I will rebuild the Grange. Don't go, Tor. Look at me.

She looked, and her face changed; she looked disgusted. Keep away, you're not wanted, know your place. A prisoner in handcuffs has no place here, you're not like us, go away. Get back to where you belong, leave us to our grieving, leave us alone.

The younger sister limped forward to throw a flower.

White flowers look grey in the rain. Farewell, elder sister, rest in peace, goodbye, don't forget us. Here is your flower, wet and grey, adieu.

Tor, look at me again, wait for me. Young sister, don't leave me on my own. I can't bear life without you, can't bear to lose you. Speak to me, say something, Tor.

'Come on, Mack, better be going.'

Mack. Mate. Jack, Chum. Life inside forced you to accept any name. You became one of the herd whatever your name was, just another of society's rejects. He was a petty larcenist with a record of grievous bodily harm. For Bonnie's sake he'd become a convicted thief, was getting his payment. Carelessness, over-ambition, over-confidence, had been his real crimes. Aunt's advice wasn't true, he didn't believe her. Ambition hadn't killed the rat; he wasn't dead, Bonnie was. Bonnie, his loving sweetheart, his dear one, was gone from him. The whole world, outside and inside, was a huge trap waiting to get you. Murderers rapists and burglars were his comrades now.

'Mack. Time to be getting back to the Villa now. Do you hear?'

You need patience and long sufferance for prison work. Ed was causing the staff extra work. There were too many villains inside, without providing escorts to funerals. They had all pitied Ed for losing his girl. He must be cuffed though, no matter what happened, couldn't risk him doing a runner with his record of GBH.

'*Mack!*'

Ed felt the tug on his wrist again.

'I must speak. Just a minute. Wait, Tor.'

'Doesn't look as if the party wants to speak to you, Mack.'

Tor was walking away now, with Ula limping behind her. He must, it was his last chance, he must drag the screw after him.

'Tor. Wait. Please.'

She spoke to him.

'*You.*'

He wanted to scream at her, he was heartsick, she must believe him. He had stolen the cash for Bonnie's sake. When he came out he would help her and her family. They were involved forever, it was meant to be. She mustn't imagine he wasn't good enough, he was changing and improving, he intended to change a lot more. They must stick together, shared memories still bound them. Bonds like that couldn't be broken. He would come back, he would help; they were conjoined.

'Come on, Mack. Back now.'

'For pete's sake, get my name right; it's not Mack, it's Ed, short for Eden. Get it right for once, can't you?'

'Sorry, Mack. I mean, Ed.'

He stood still, his head was lowered now, the rain was blinding him, but he wasn't beaten, he'd fight till he died. They belonged to him, he belonged to them, it wasn't over.

He heard the footsteps in the wet behind him, slicking over the grass, he felt the hand touching him, he smelled that perfume again, familiar as cake, sickly-sweet, cloying, foul. ('Be content with your lot. Ambition killed the rat.')

'Ed. I couldn't get here any sooner. I'm here now. Right? Poor old Bonn, silly bitch. Fancy doing that to herself with a knitting needle. Nasty. Dangerous. I warned her not to, silly cow.'

'You shouldn't of come. Why did you? You shouldn't of . . .'

'Stop away from Bonn's funeral? Not me. Not after all we been through. A right miserable misery you are. You didn't have to half kill that copper what was bringing you in. Why didn't you go quietly? If you had, you wouldn't be inside now.

'I was trying to help Bonnie. I did it for Bonnie. I loved Bonnie.'

'Yeah. 'Course. I know that. Shame. I'm here ready and

waiting when you're out again, same as always. Red and Ed, back in harness, ready for our arrangement. Long time no hear, no see.'